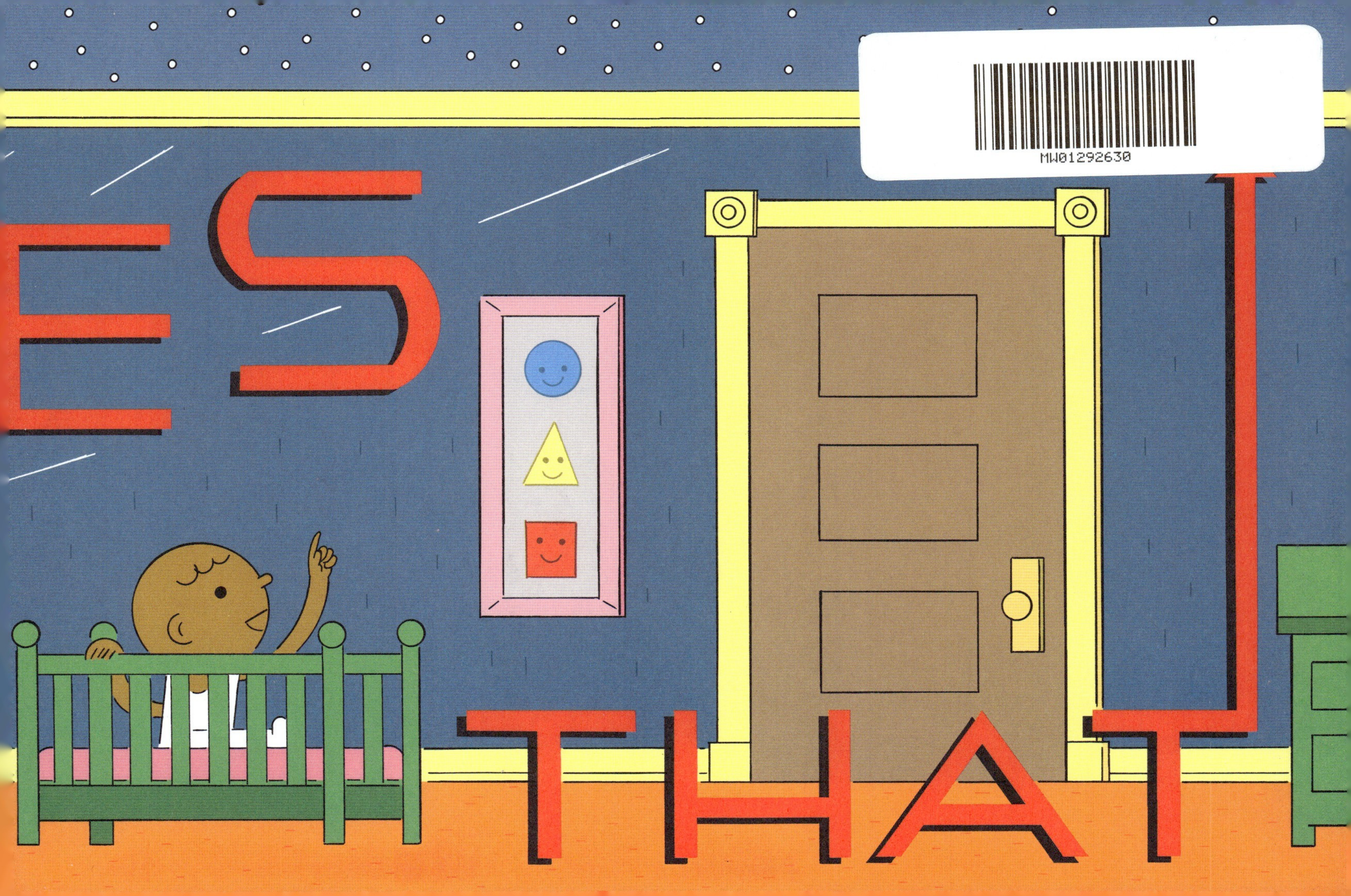
ES
THAT

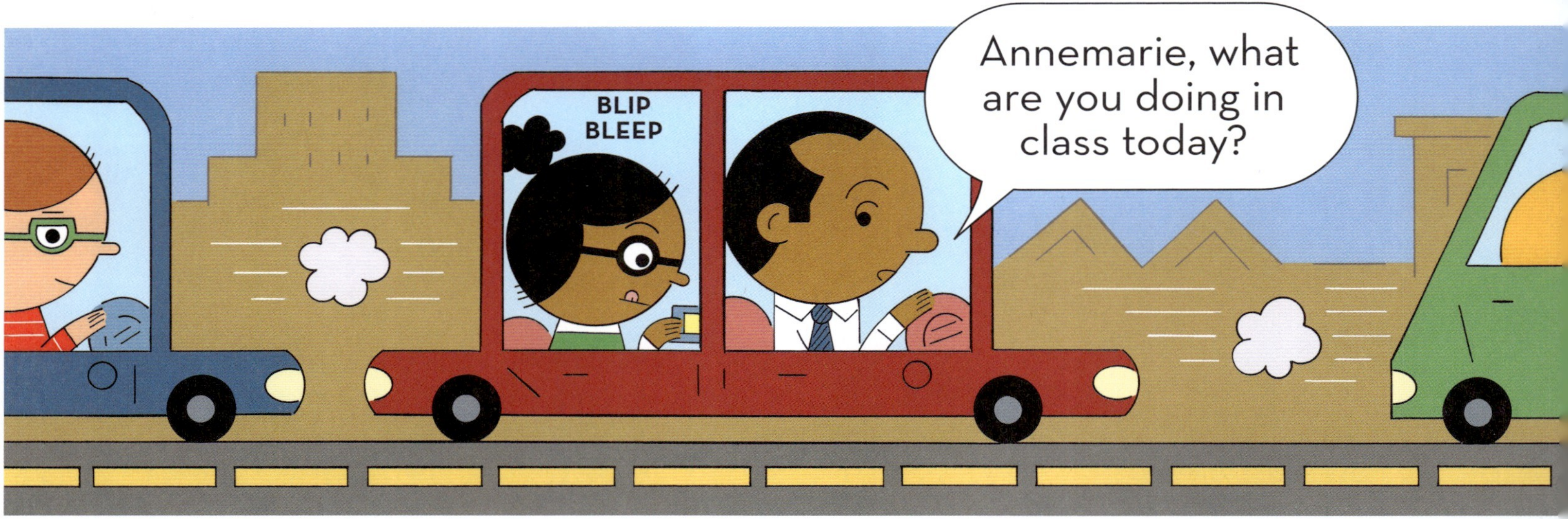
BLIP
BLEEP
Annemarie, what are you doing in class today?

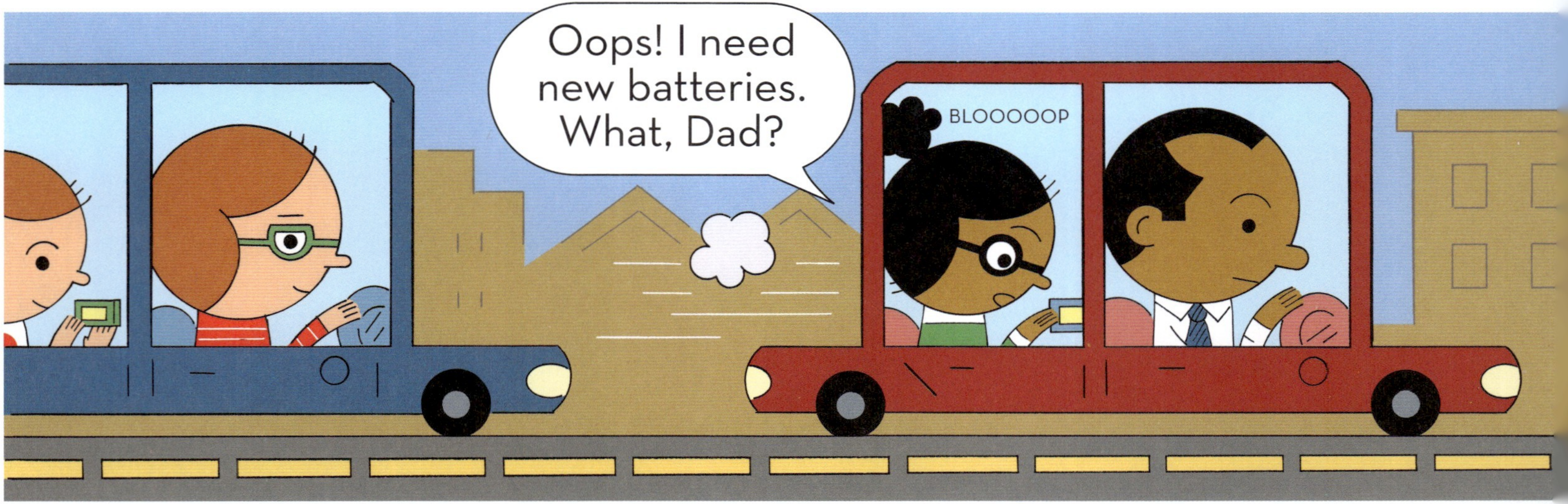
Oops! I need new batteries. What, Dad?
BLOOOOOP

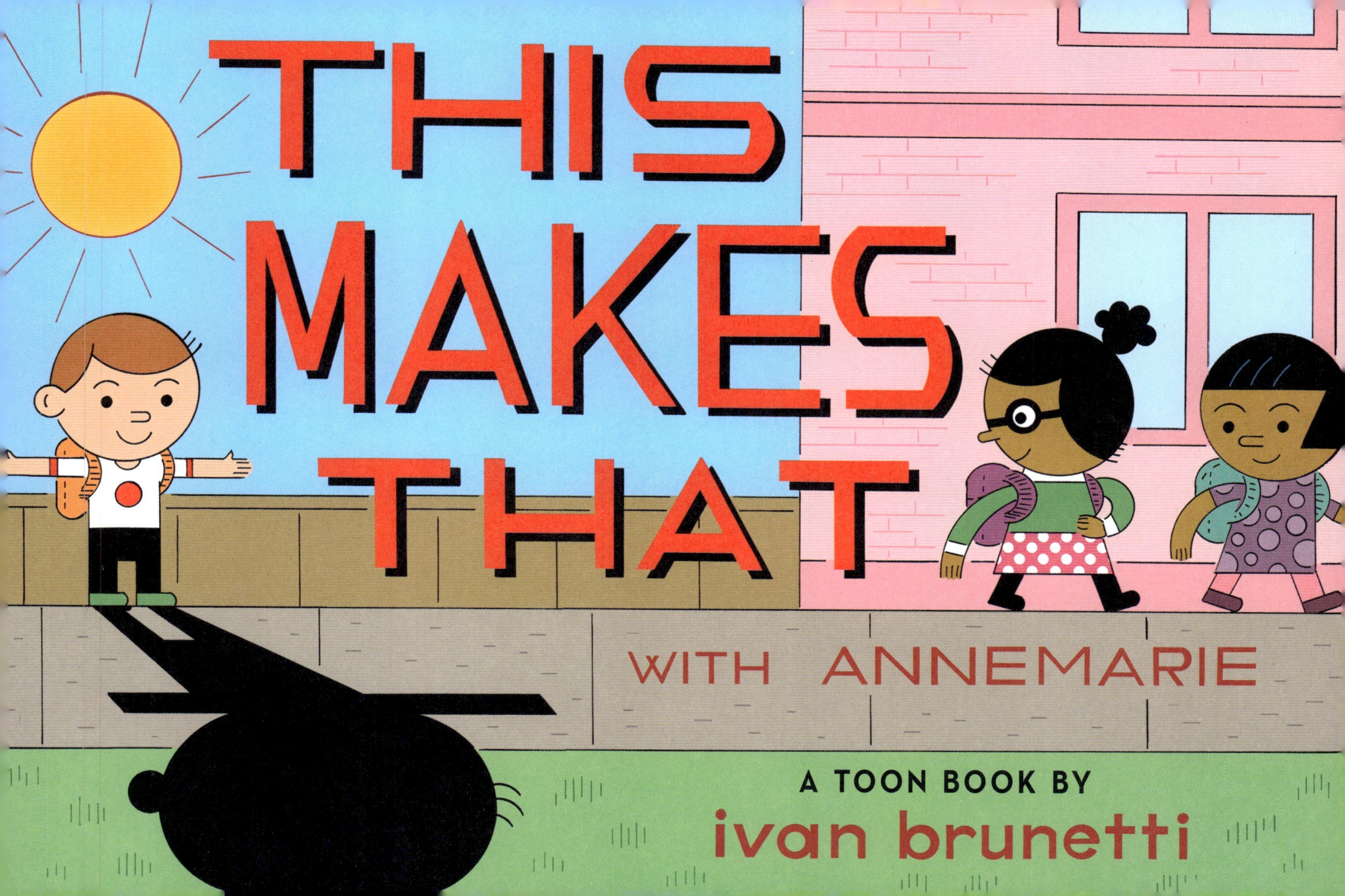
THIS MAKES THAT
WITH ANNEMARIE
A TOON BOOK BY
ivan brunetti

Make sure to look for the other TOON Books by the same author:
Wordplay, **3x4**, **Shapes and Shapes**, and **Comics: Easy as ABC!**

For Laura

Editorial Director: FRANÇOISE MOULY

Book Design: IVAN BRUNETTI & FRANÇOISE MOULY

IVAN BRUNETTI's artwork was done in India ink and colored digitally.

A TOON Book™ © 2025 Ivan Brunetti & TOON Books, an imprint of Astra Books for Young Readers, a division of Astra Publishing House. Copying or digitizing this book for storage, display, or distribution in any other medium is strictly prohibited. All rights reserved. For information about permission to reproduce selections from this book, please contact permissions@astrapublishinghouse.com. TOON Books®, TOON Graphics™, and TOON Into Reading!™ are trademarks of Astra Publishing House. Library of Congress Cataloging-in-Publication Data: Names: Brunetti, Ivan, author, illustrator. Title: This makes that : with Annemarie / Ivan Brunetti. Description: New York : TOON Books, 2025. | Summary: A diverse group of elementary school students play with STEAM concepts in a classroom Makerspace, experimenting with a lemon battery, a baking-soda rocket, ice cream, and much more! Identifiers: LCCN 2024036762 (print) | LCCN 2024036763 (ebook) | ISBN 9781662665561 (hardback) | ISBN 9781662665585 (epub) Subjects: CYAC: Graphic novels. | Schools--Fiction | Makerspaces--Fiction. | LCGFT: Graphic novels. Classification: LCC PZ7.7.B813 Th 2025 (print) | LCC PZ7.7.B813 (ebook) | DDC 7.41.5/973 [E]--dc23/eng20241007 LC record available at https://lccn.loc.gov/2024036762 All our books are Smyth Sewn (the highest library-quality binding available) and printed with soy-based inks on acid-free, woodfree paper harvested from responsible sources. Printed in China. First edition.

ISBN 978-1-6626-6556-1 (hardcover)

10 9 8 7 6 5 4 3 2 1

WWW.TOON-BOOKS.COM

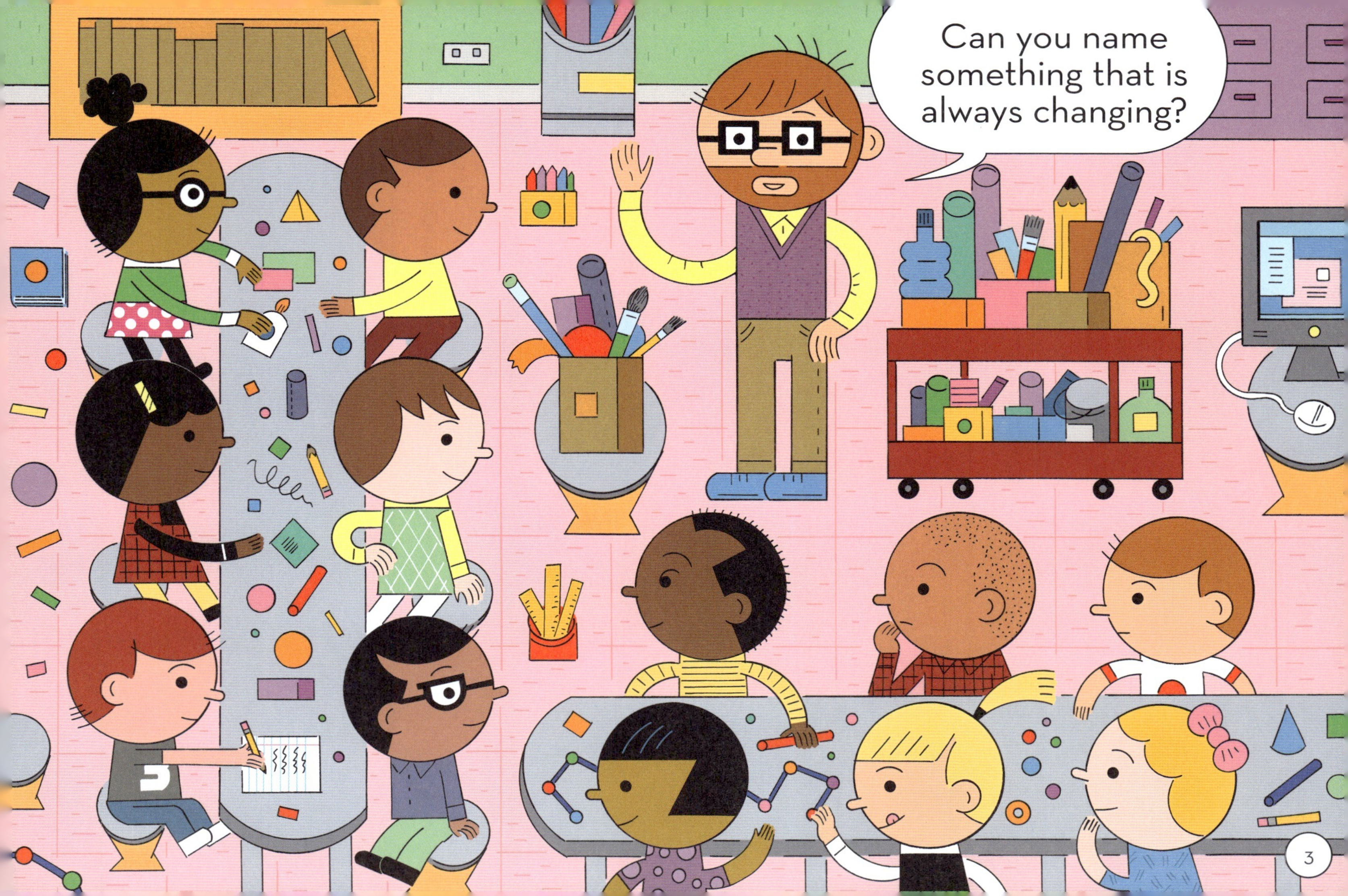
Can you name something that is always changing?

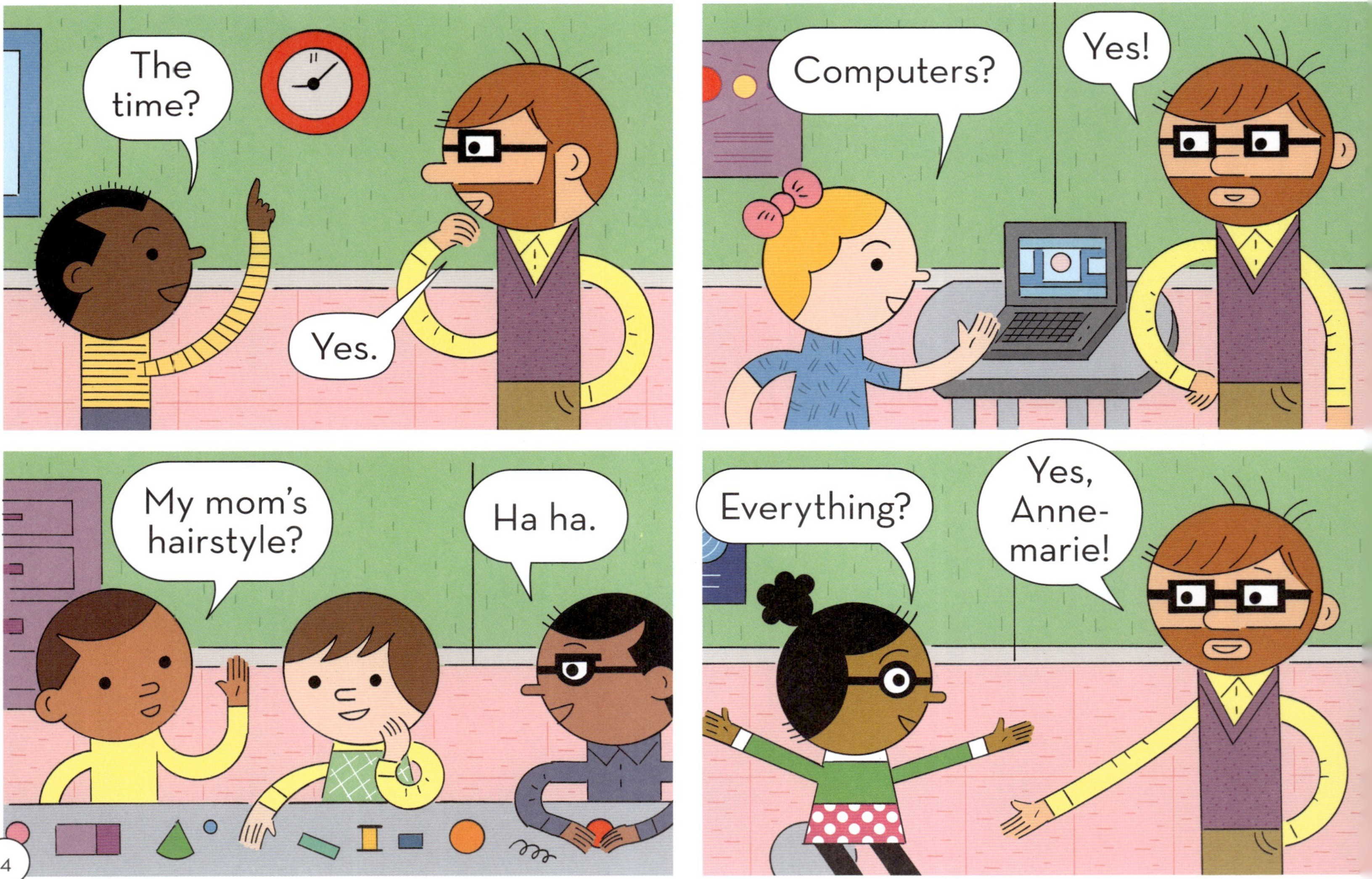
The time?
Yes.
Computers?
Yes!
My mom's hairstyle?
Ha ha.
Everything?
Yes, Anne-marie!

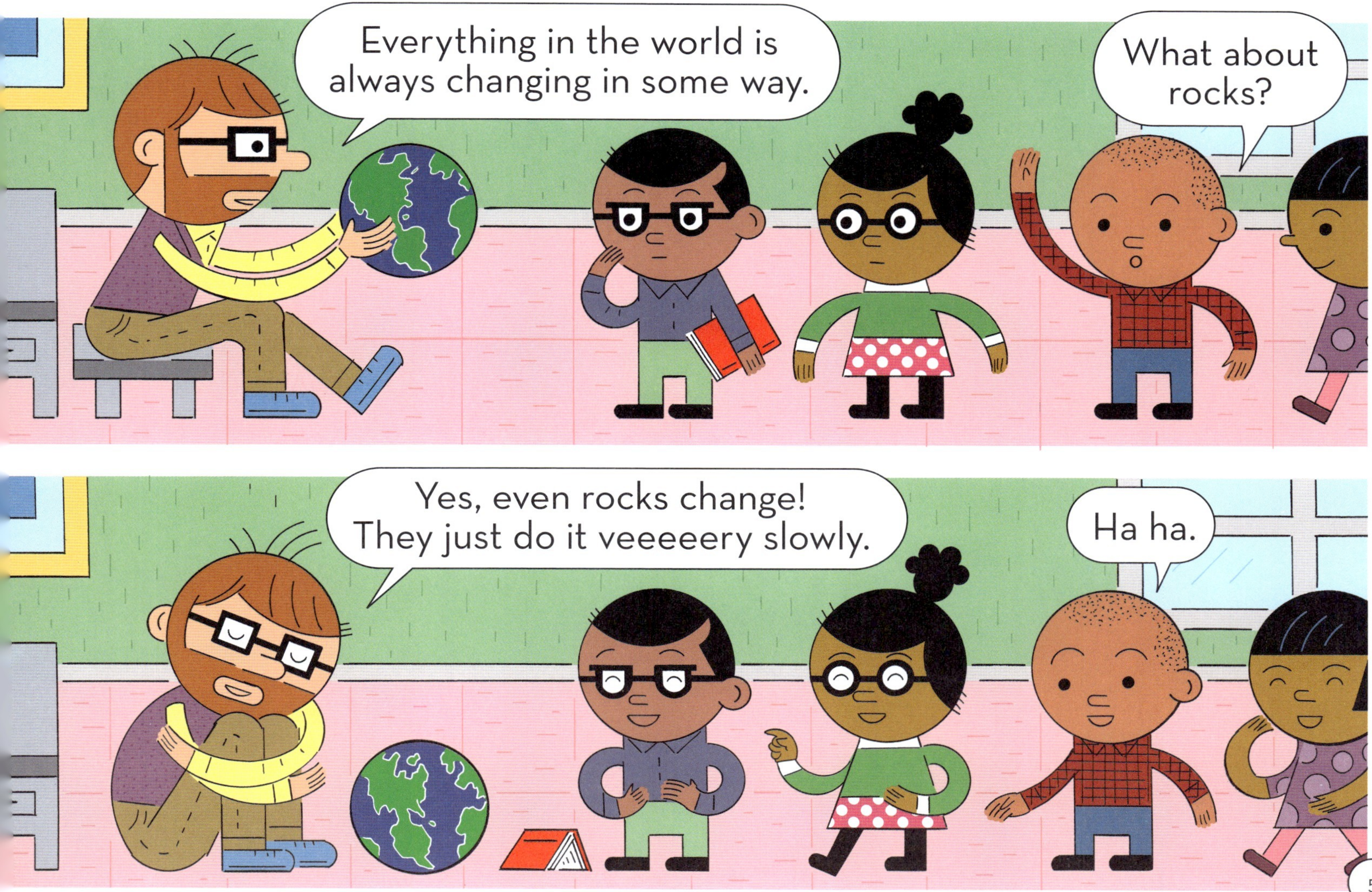
Everything in the world is always changing in some way.
What about rocks?
Yes, even rocks change! They just do it veeeeery slowly.
Ha ha.

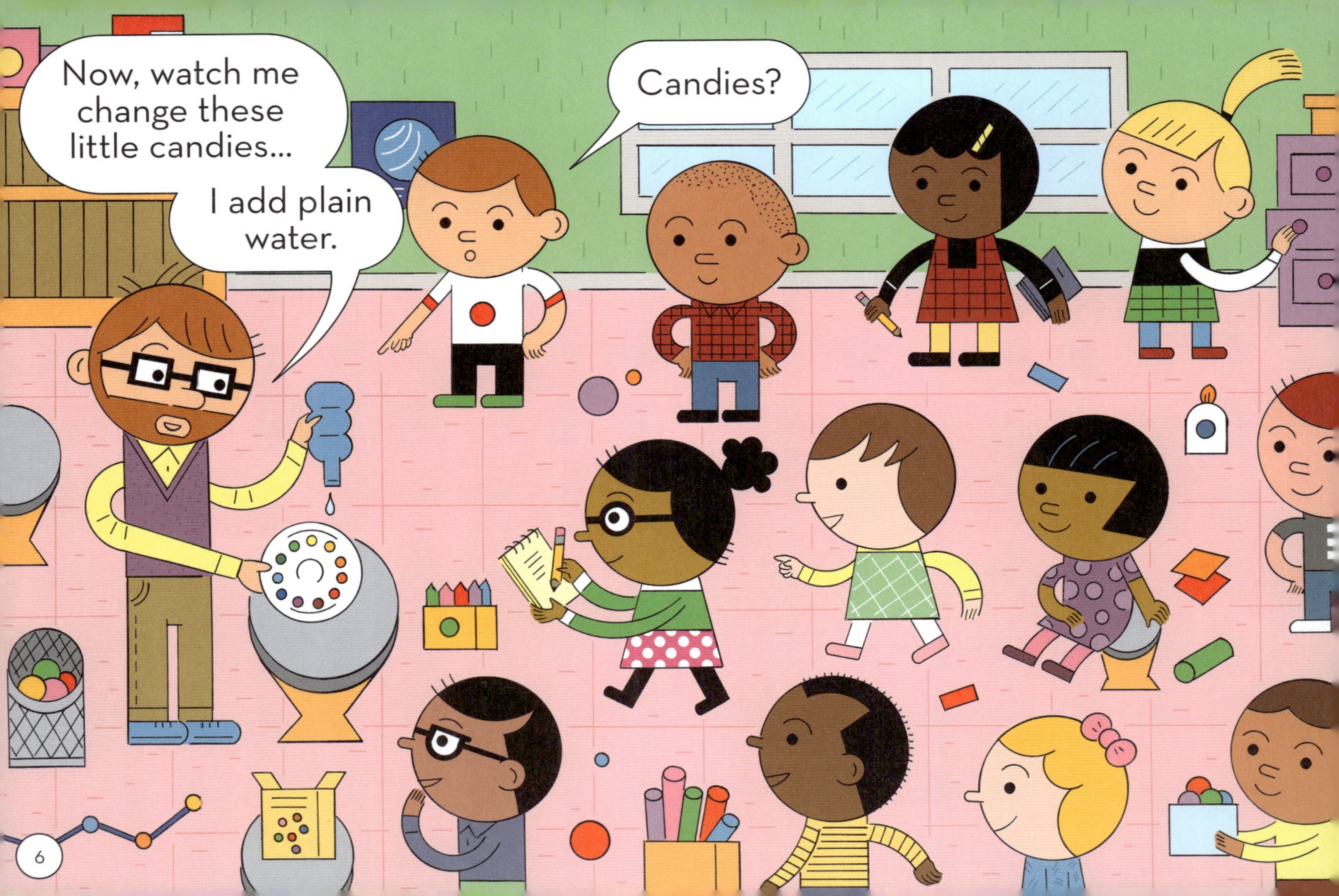
Now, watch me change these little candies...
I add plain water.
Candies?

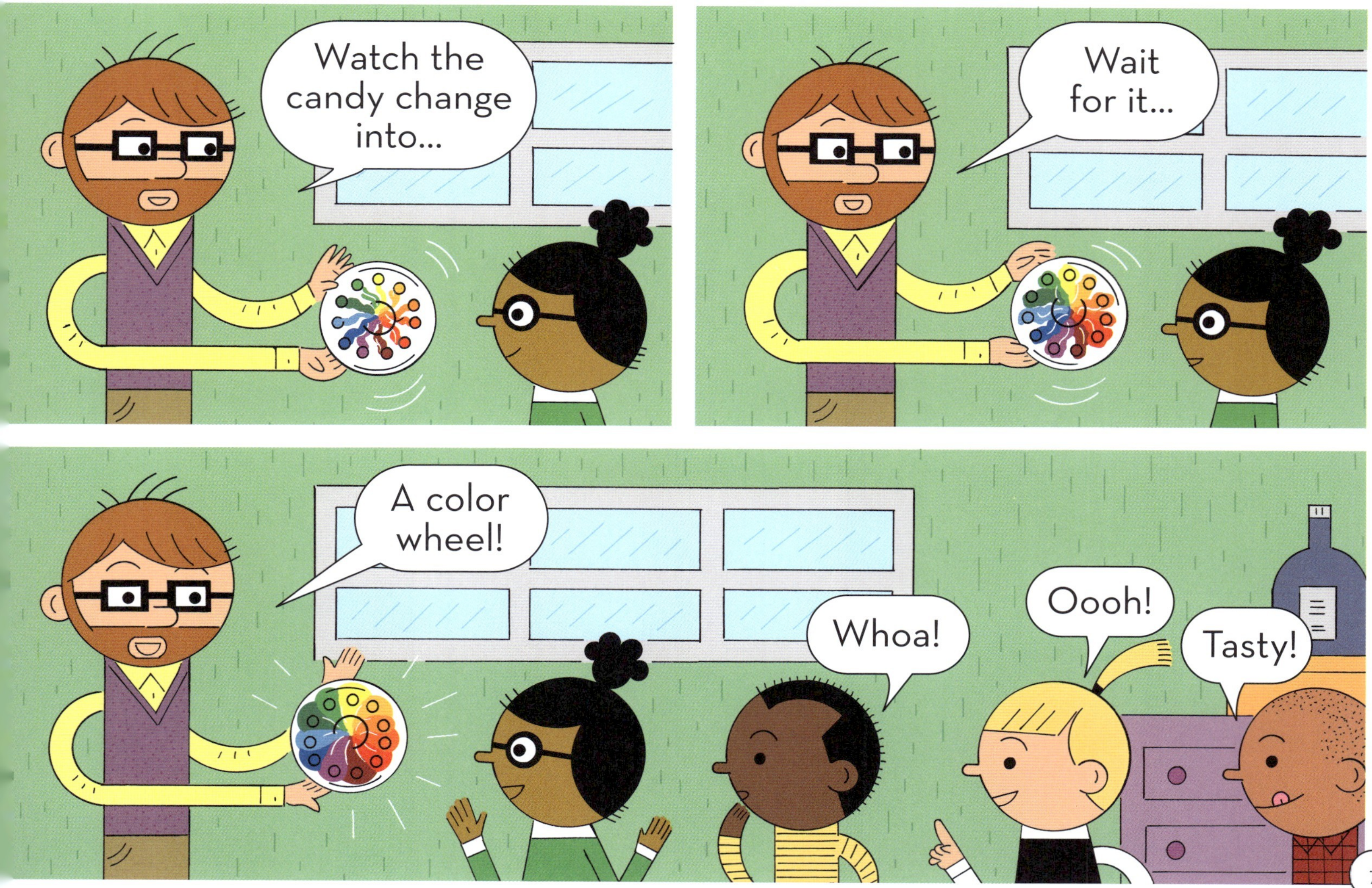
Watch the candy change into...
Wait for it...
A color wheel!
Whoa!
Oooh!
Tasty!

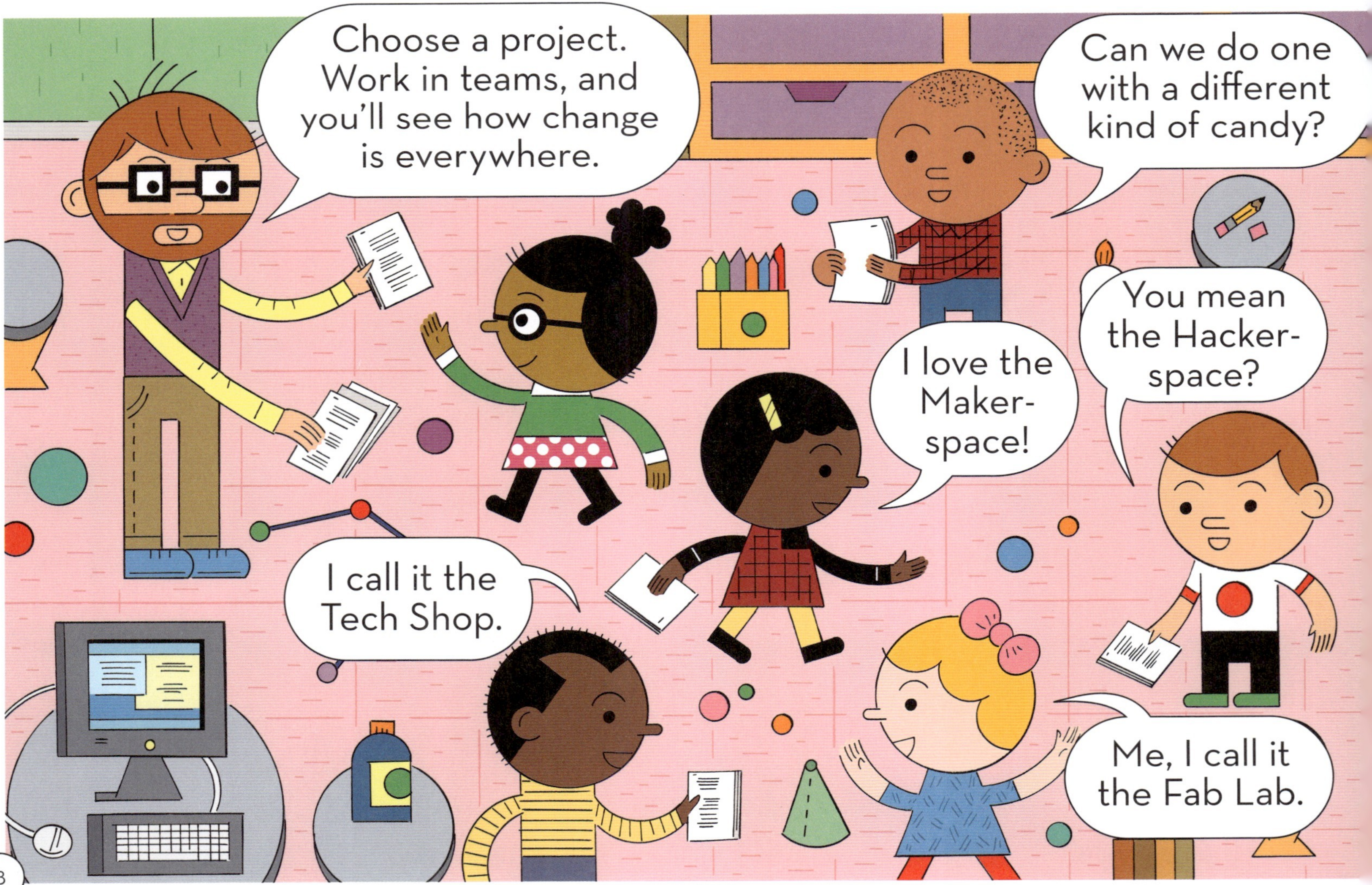
Choose a project. Work in teams, and you'll see how change is everywhere.
Can we do one with a different kind of candy?
I love the Maker-space!
You mean the Hacker-space?
I call it the Tech Shop.
Me, I call it the Fab Lab.

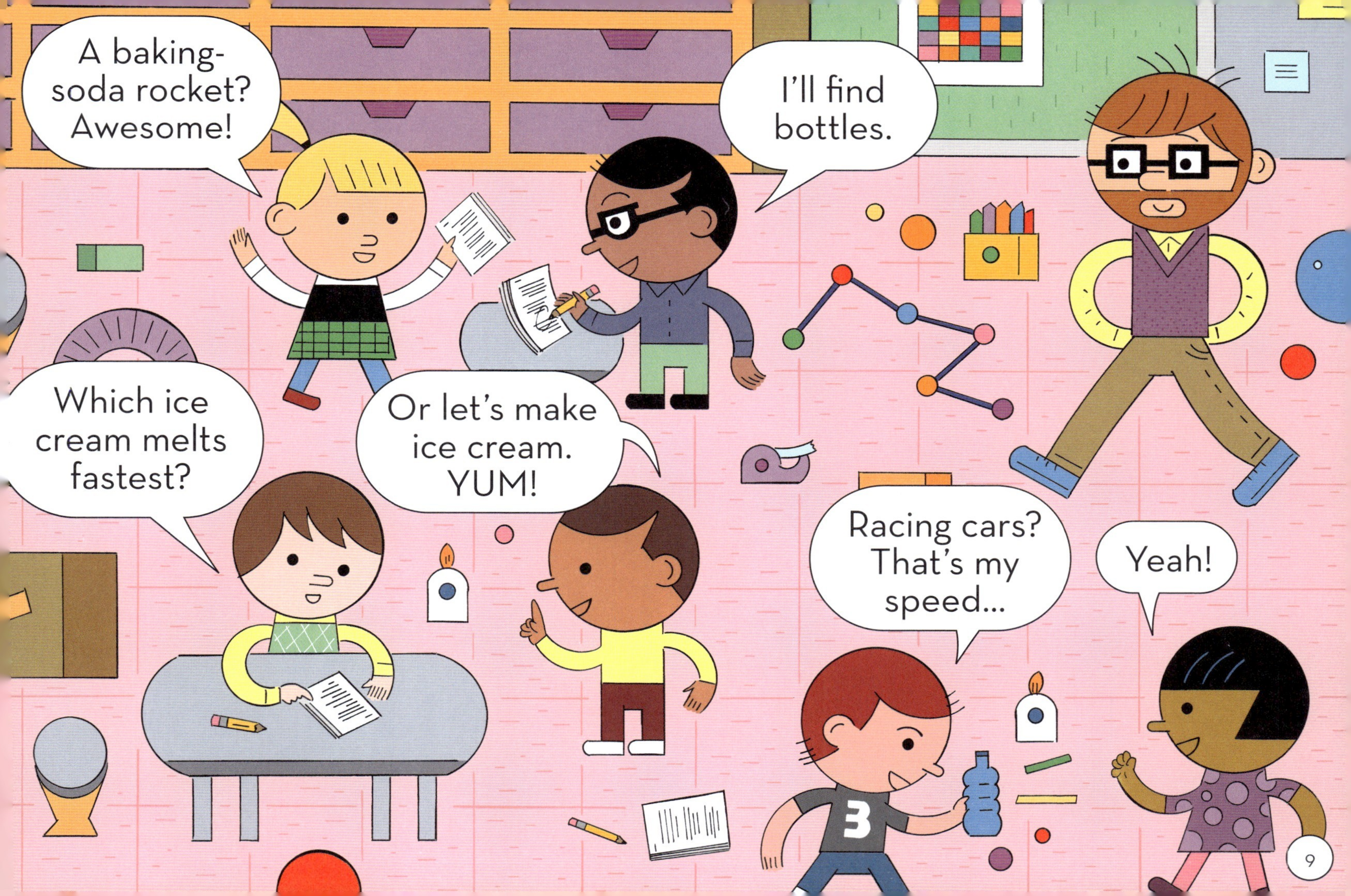
A baking-soda rocket? Awesome!
I'll find bottles.
Which ice cream melts fastest?
Or let's make ice cream. YUM!
Racing cars? That's my speed...
Yeah!

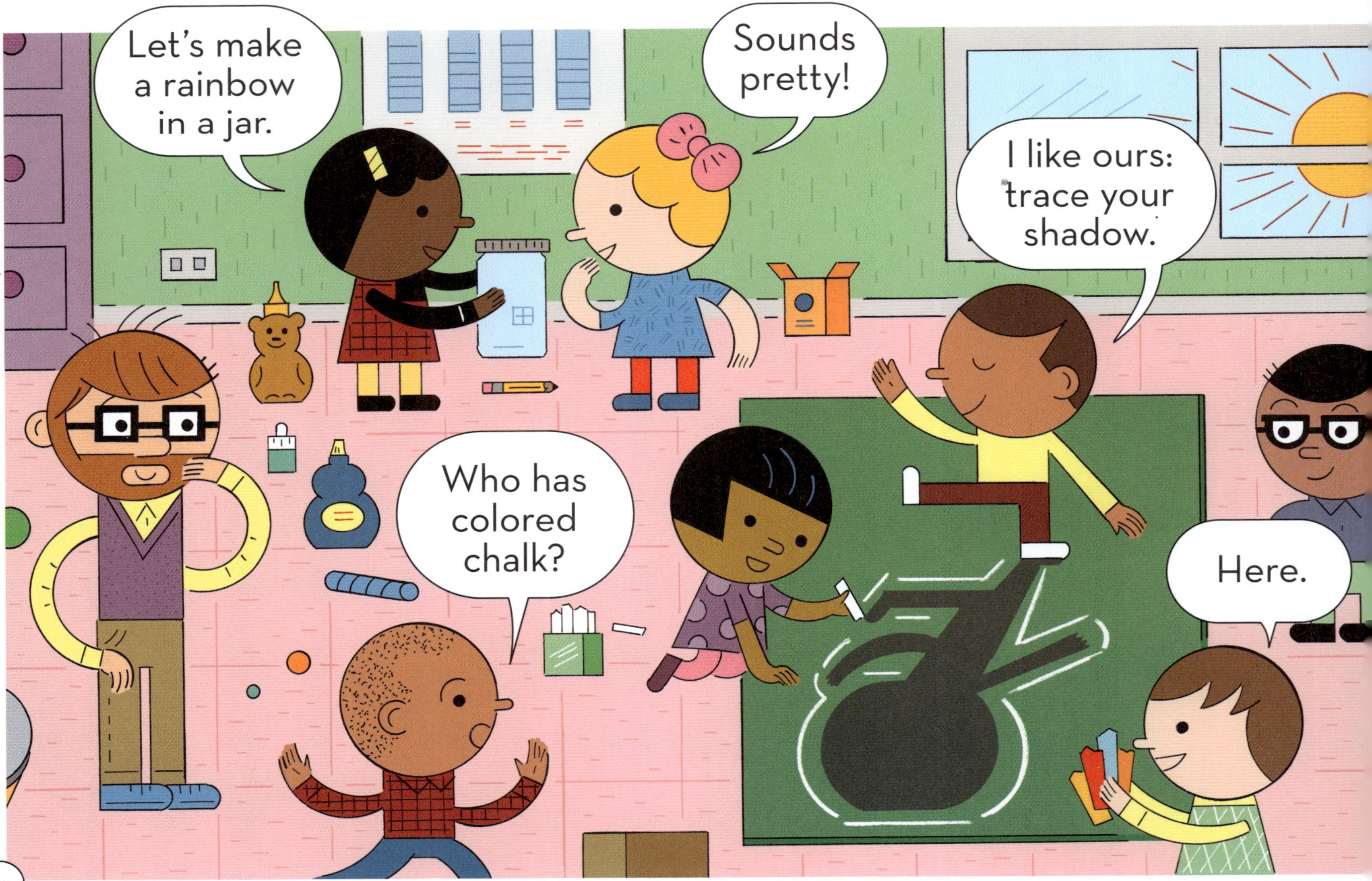
Let's make a rainbow in a jar.
Sounds pretty!
I like ours: trace your shadow.
Who has colored chalk?
Here.

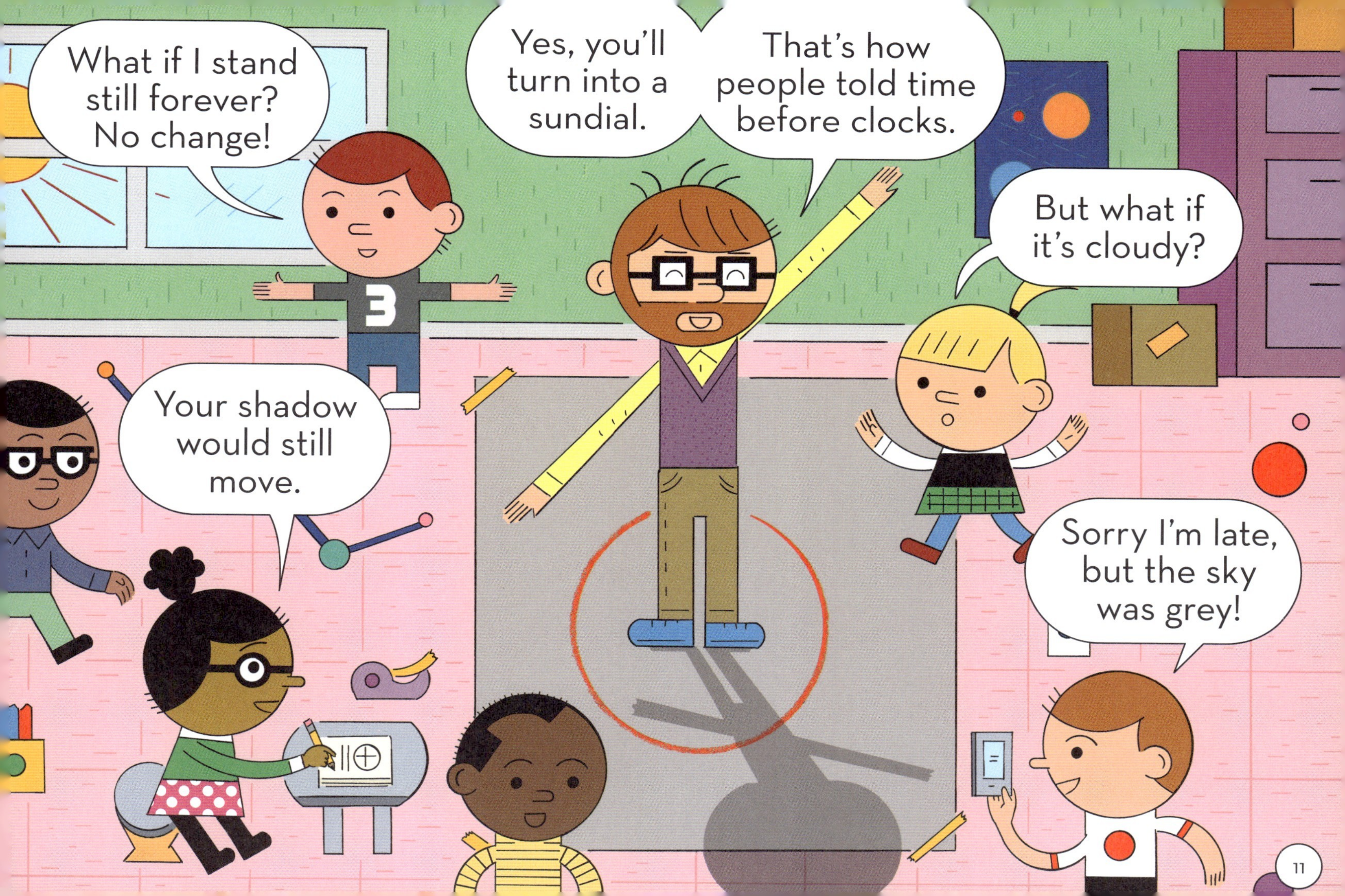
What if I stand still forever? No change!
Your shadow would still move.
Yes, you'll turn into a sundial.
That's how people told time before clocks.
But what if it's cloudy?
Sorry I'm late, but the sky was grey!
3

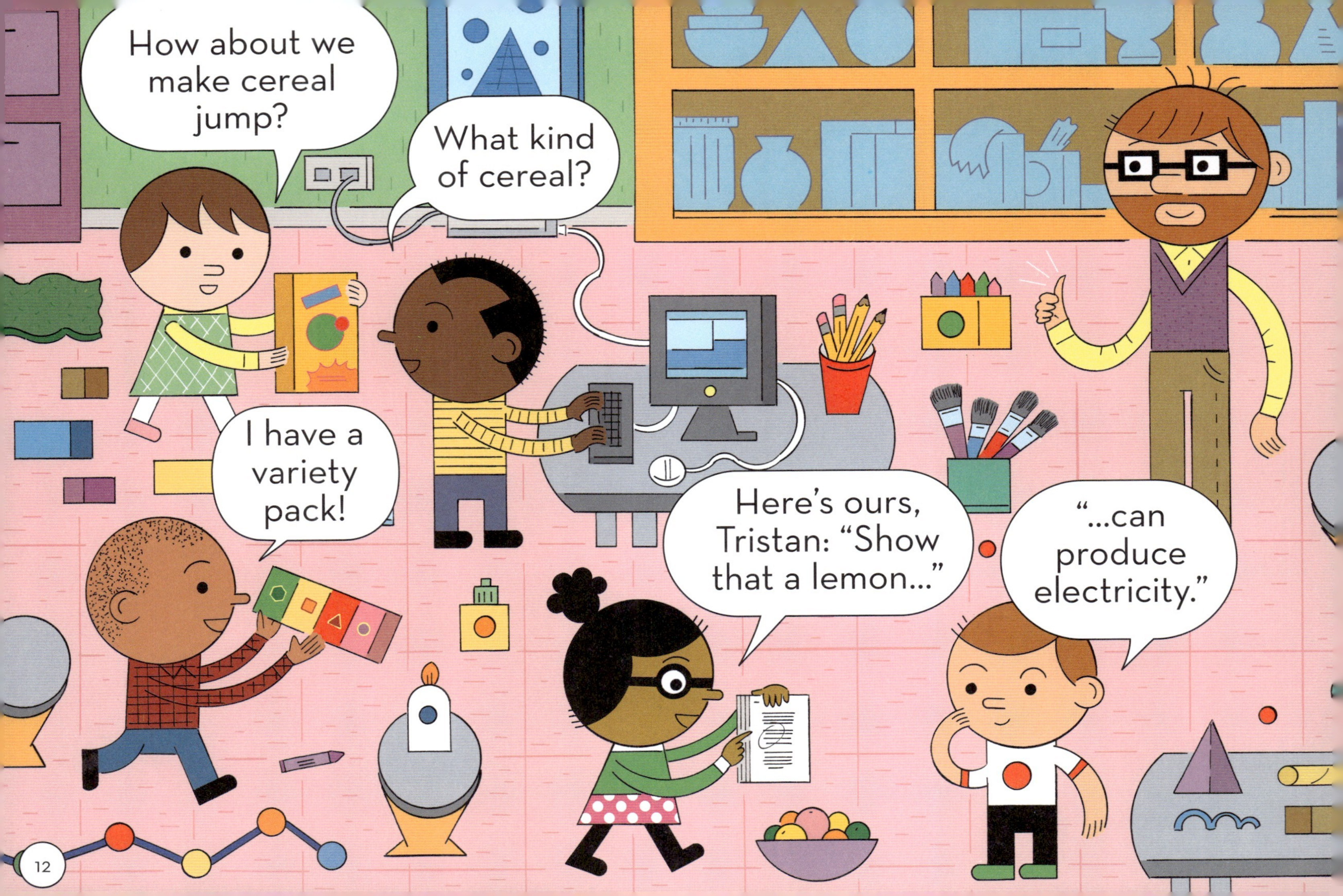
How about we make cereal jump?
What kind of cereal?
I have a variety pack!
Here's ours, Tristan: "Show that a lemon..."
"...can produce electricity."

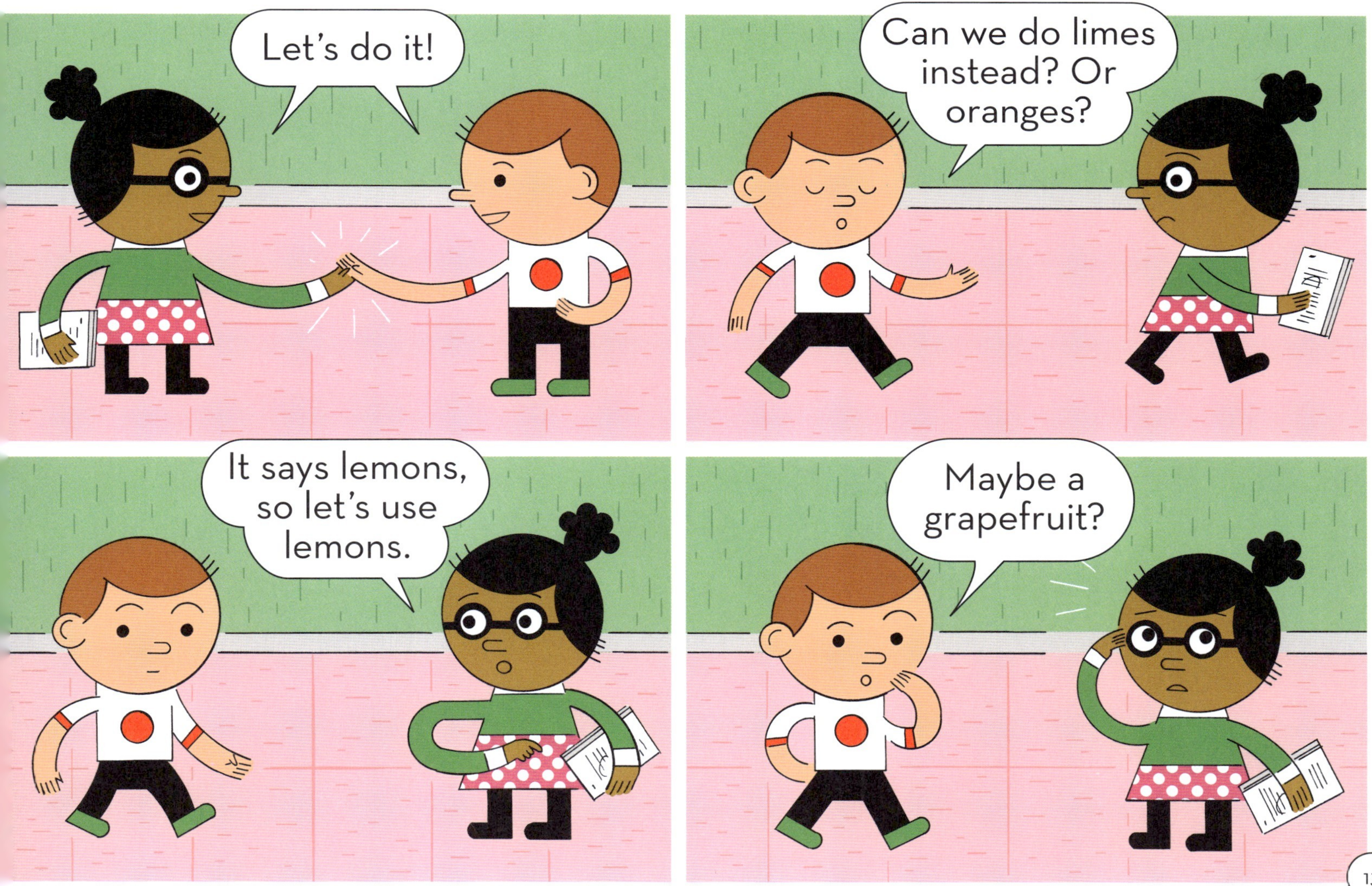
Let's do it!
Can we do limes instead? Or oranges?
It says lemons, so let's use lemons.
Maybe a grapefruit?

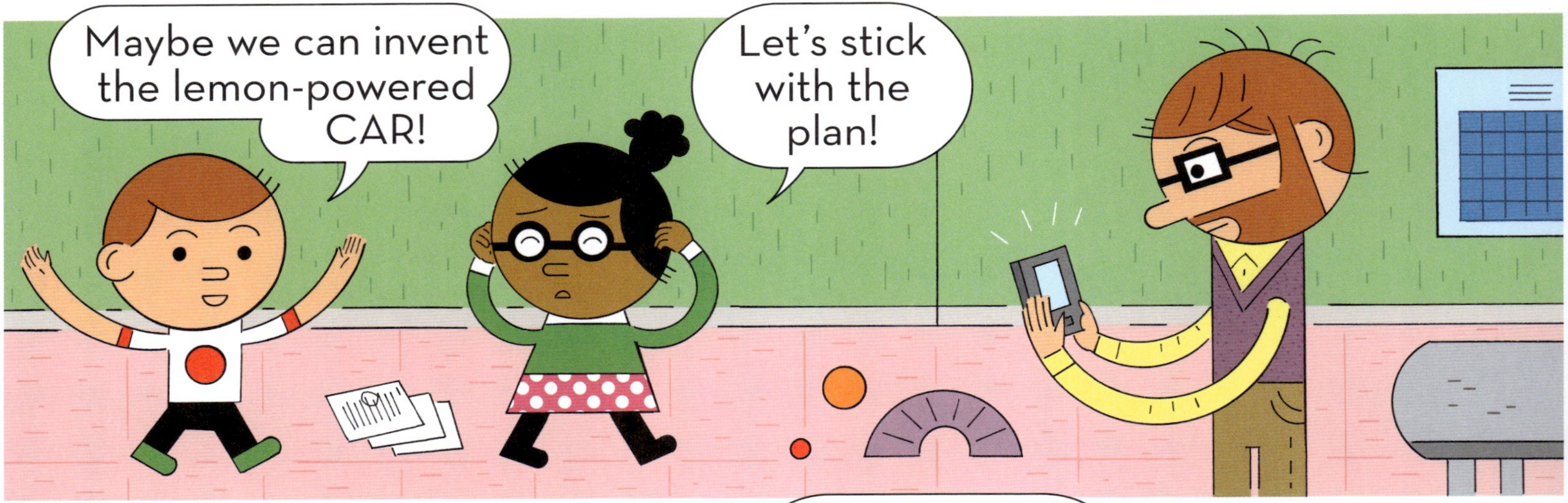
Maybe we can invent the lemon-powered CAR!
Let's stick with the plan!

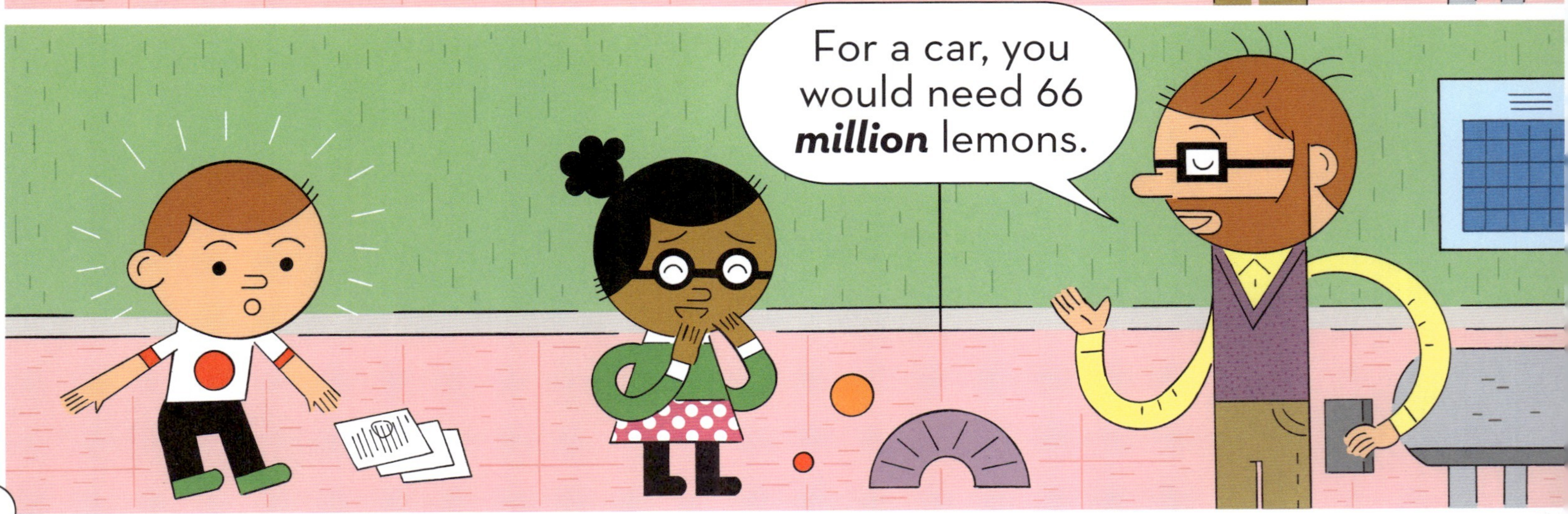
For a car, you would need 66 ***million*** lemons.

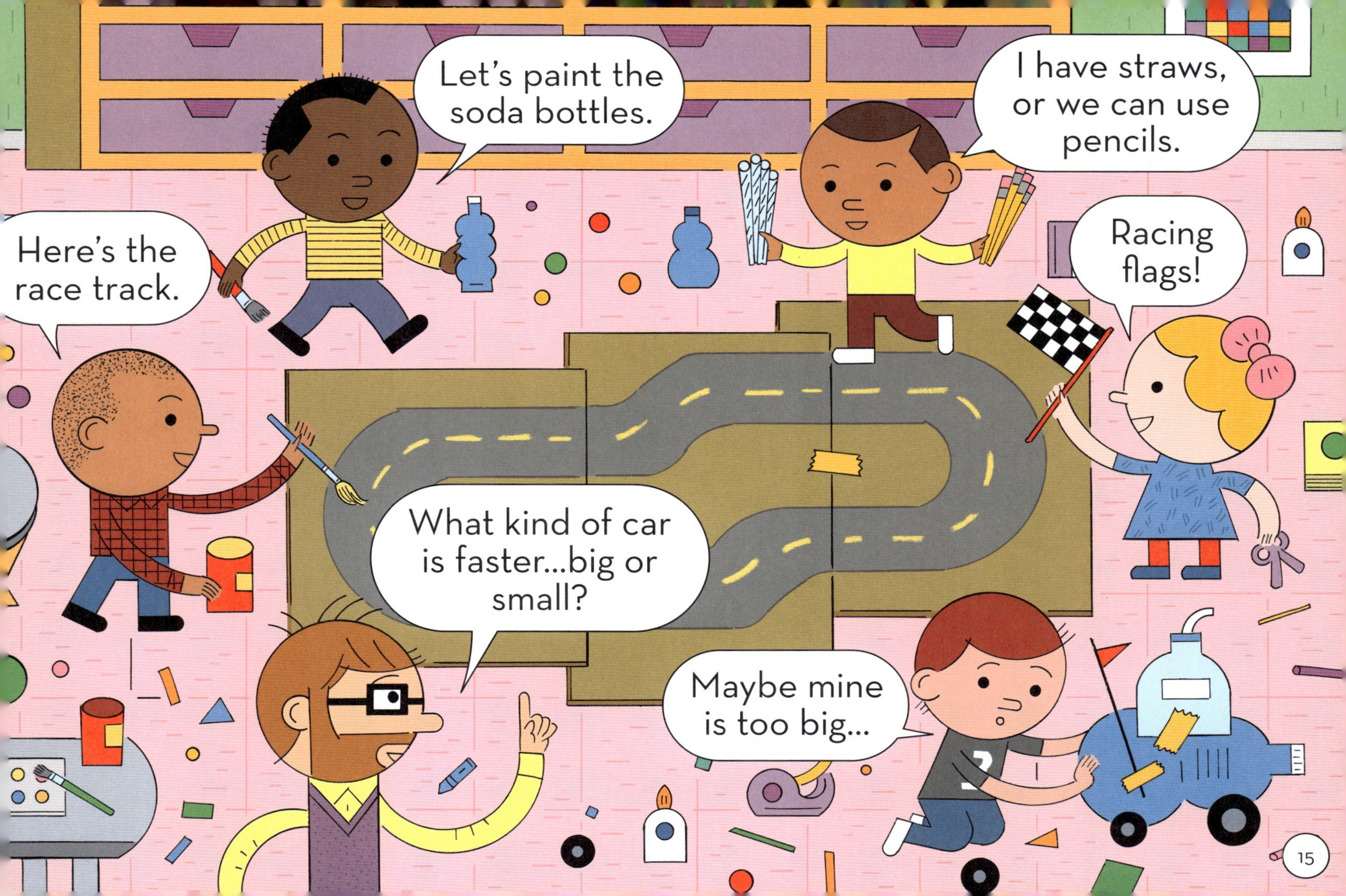
Let's paint the soda bottles.
I have straws, or we can use pencils.
Here's the race track.
Racing flags!
What kind of car is faster...big or small?
Maybe mine is too big...

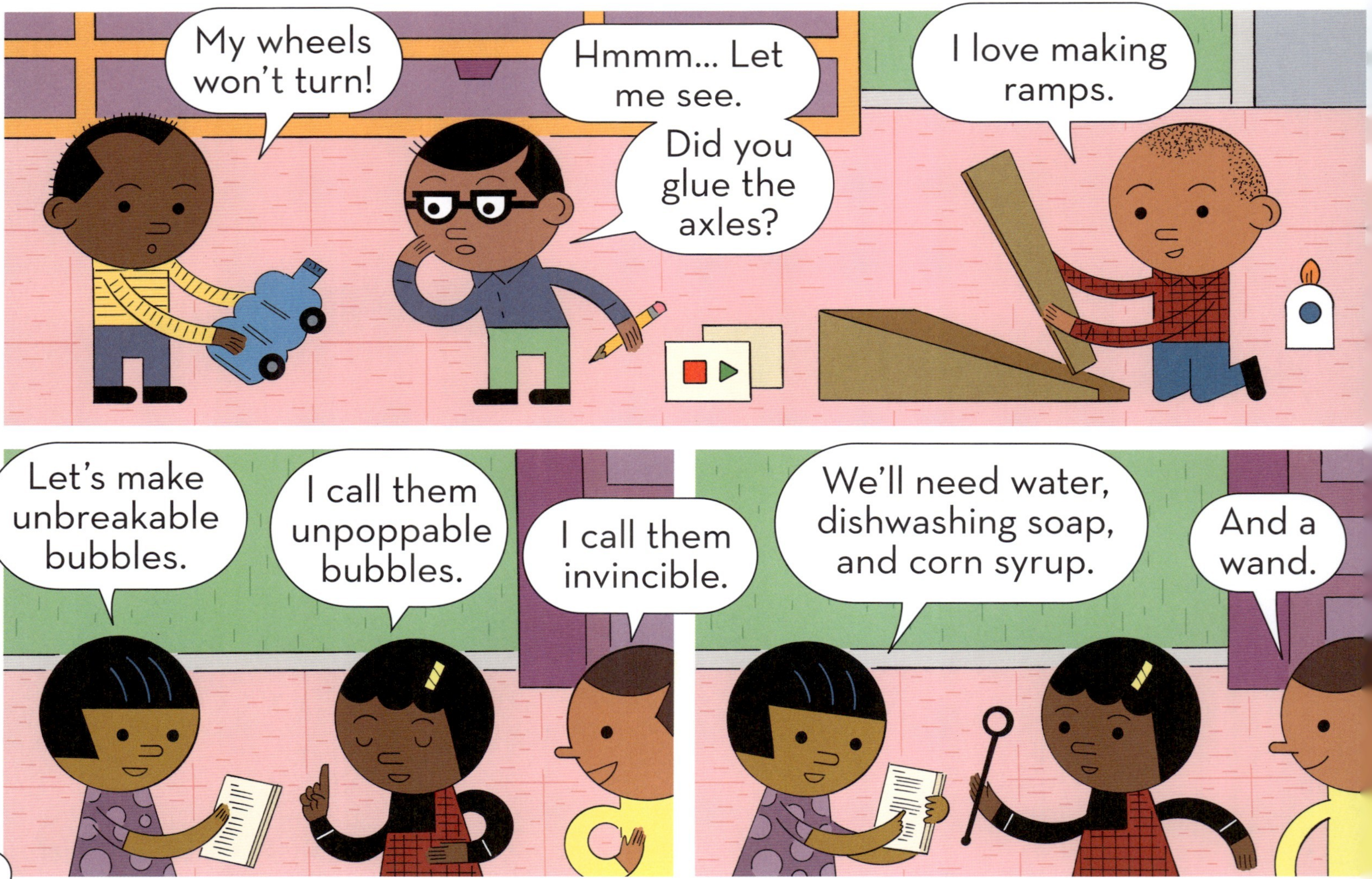
My wheels won't turn!
Hmmm... Let me see.
Did you glue the axles?
I love making ramps.
Let's make unbreakable bubbles.
I call them unpoppable bubbles.
I call them invincible.
We'll need water, dishwashing soap, and corn syrup.
And a wand.

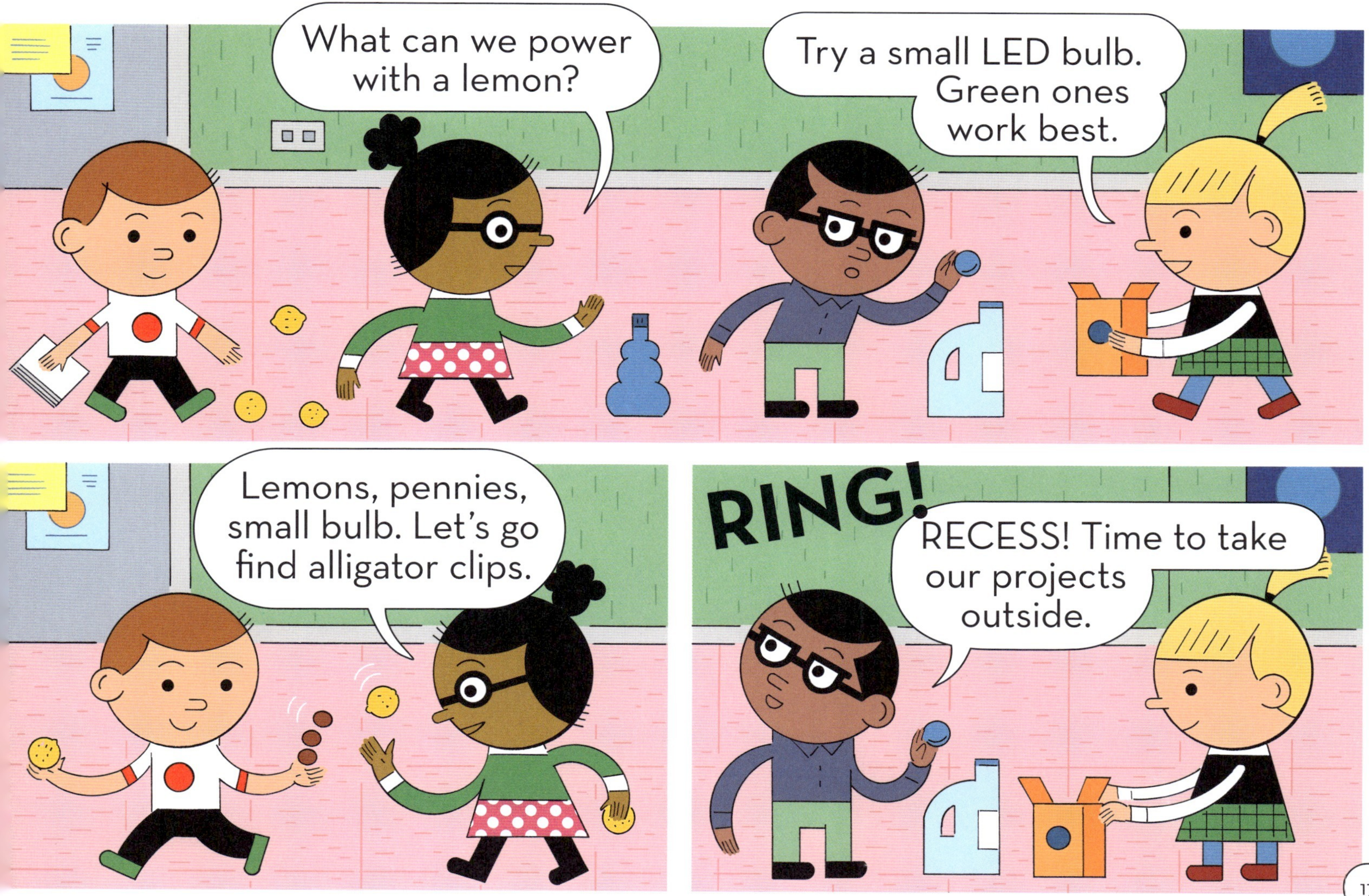
What can we power with a lemon?
Try a small LED bulb. Green ones work best.
Lemons, pennies, small bulb. Let's go find alligator clips.
RING!
RECESS! Time to take our projects outside.

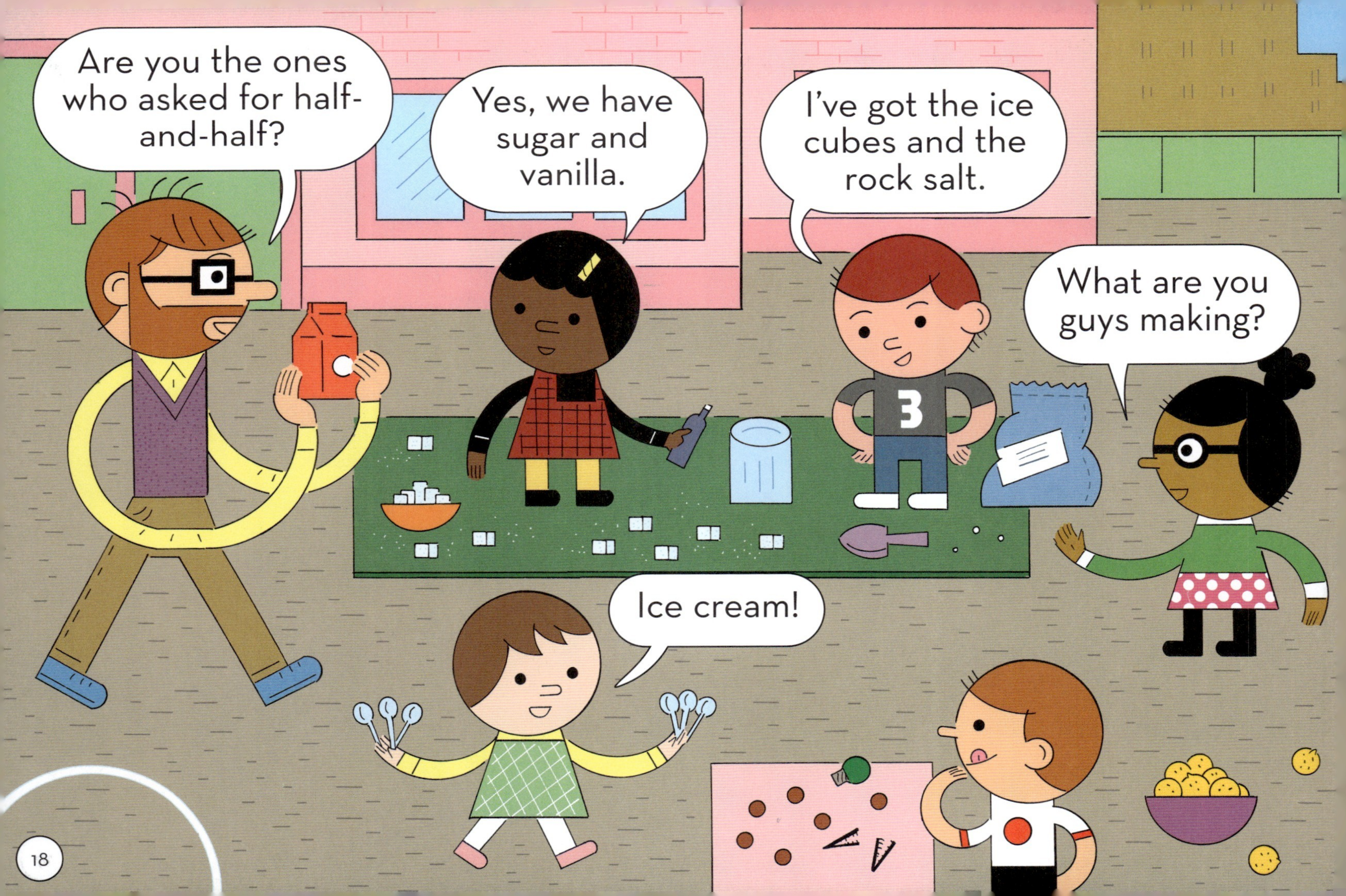
Are you the ones who asked for half-and-half?
Yes, we have sugar and vanilla.
I've got the ice cubes and the rock salt.
What are you guys making?
Ice cream!

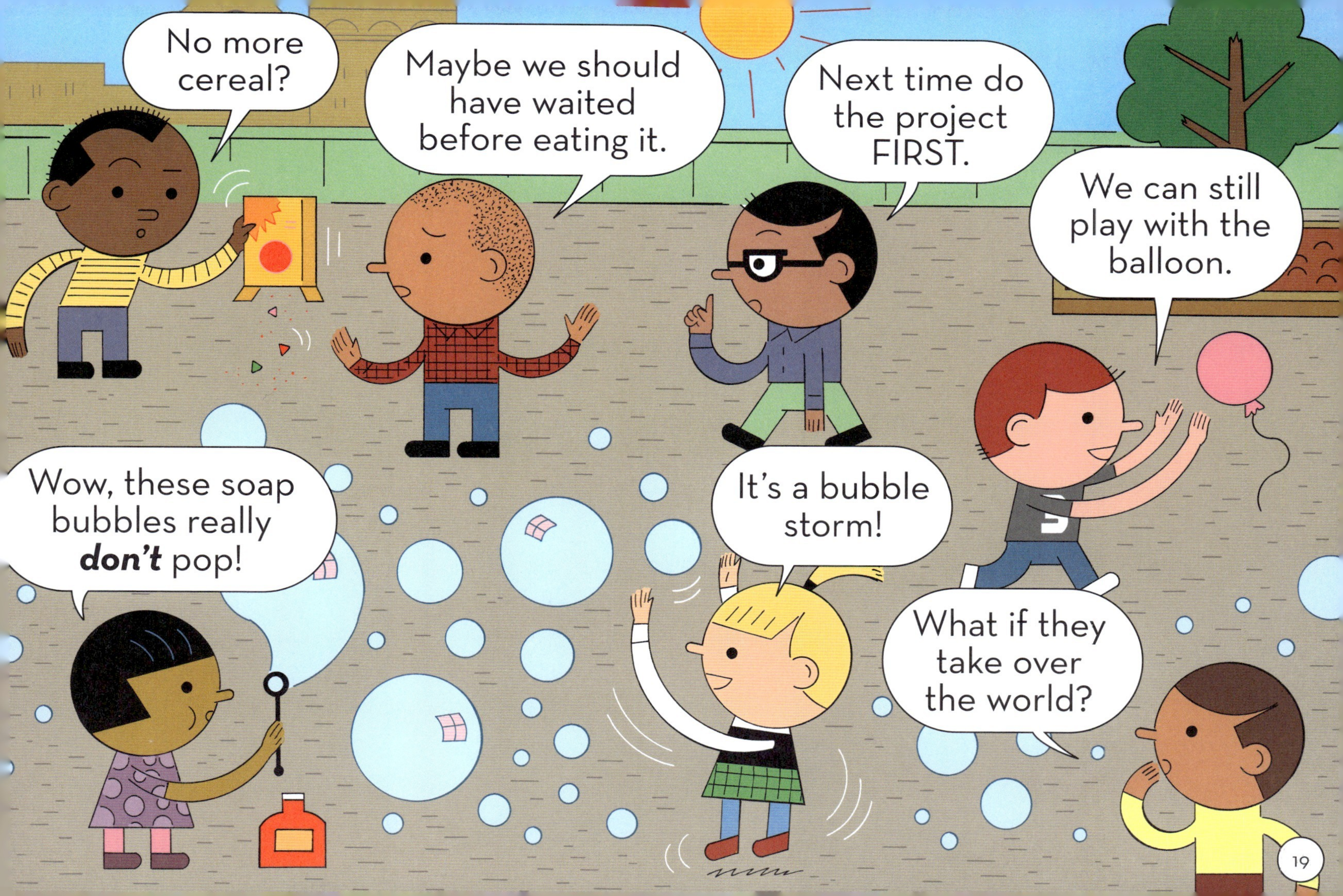
No more cereal?
Maybe we should have waited before eating it.
Next time do the project FIRST.
We can still play with the balloon.
Wow, these soap bubbles really ***don't*** pop!
It's a bubble storm!
What if they take over the world?

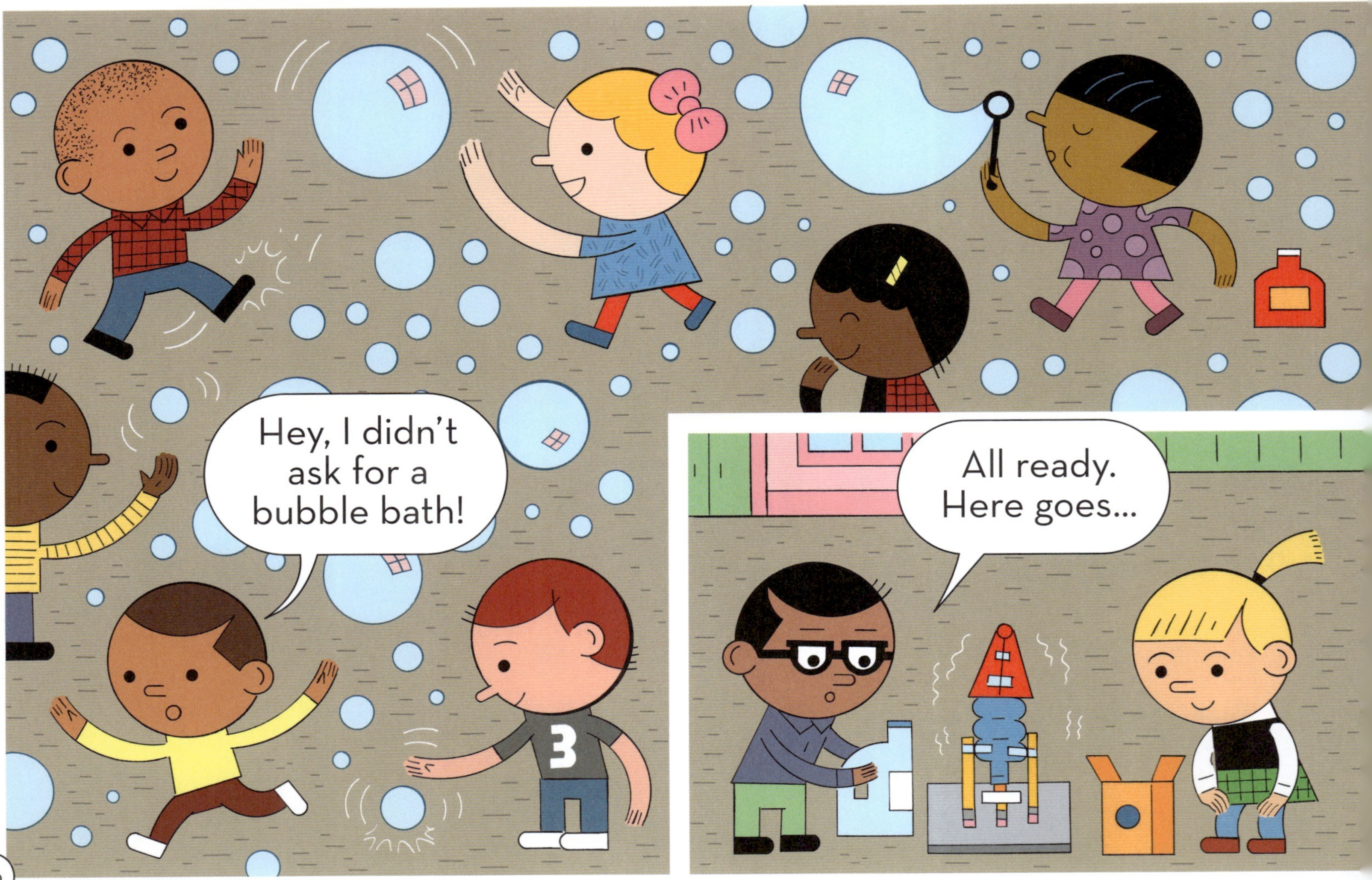
Hey, I didn't ask for a bubble bath!
All ready. Here goes...
3

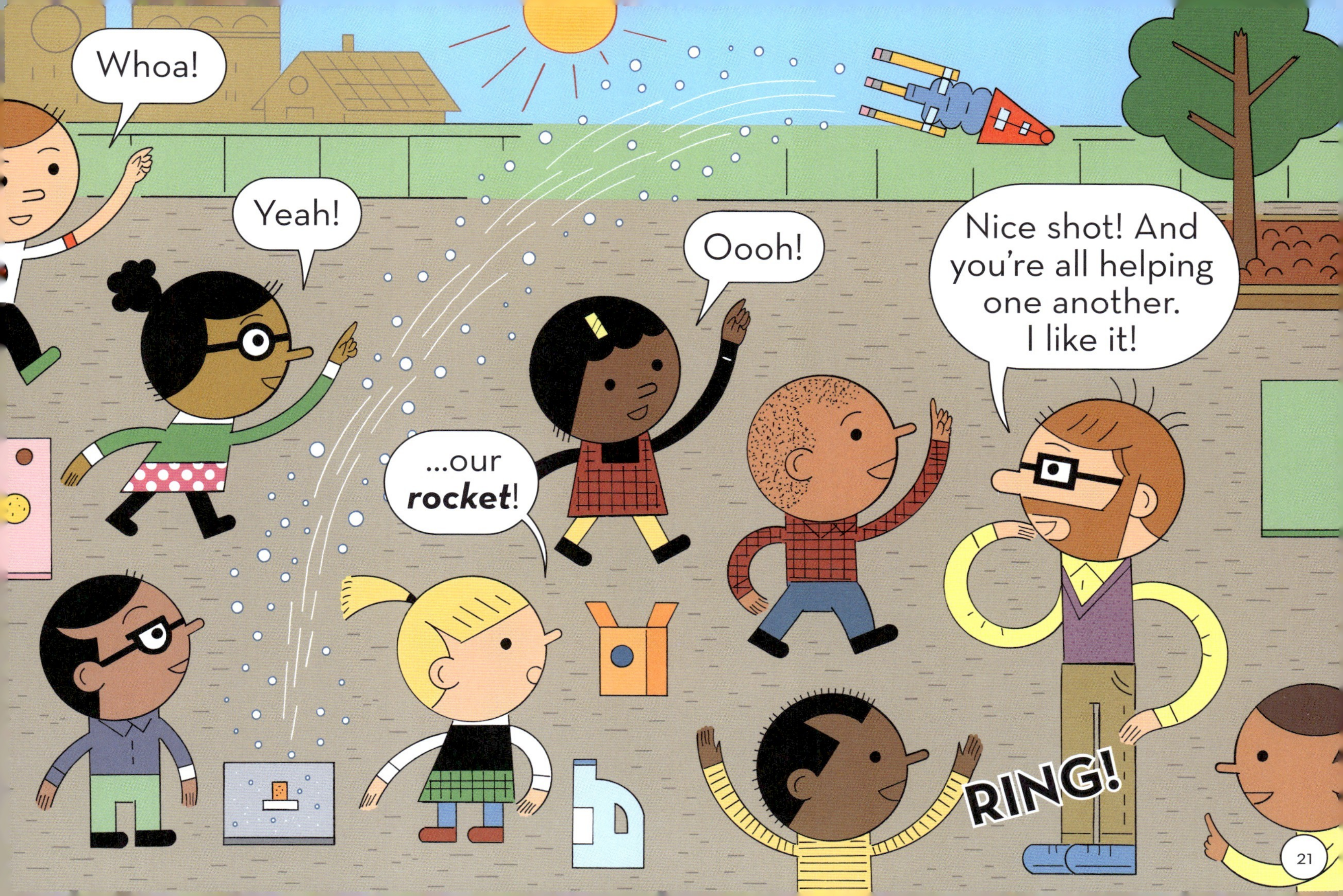
Whoa!
Yeah!
Ooh!
...our **rocket**!
Nice shot! And you're all helping one another. I like it!
RING!

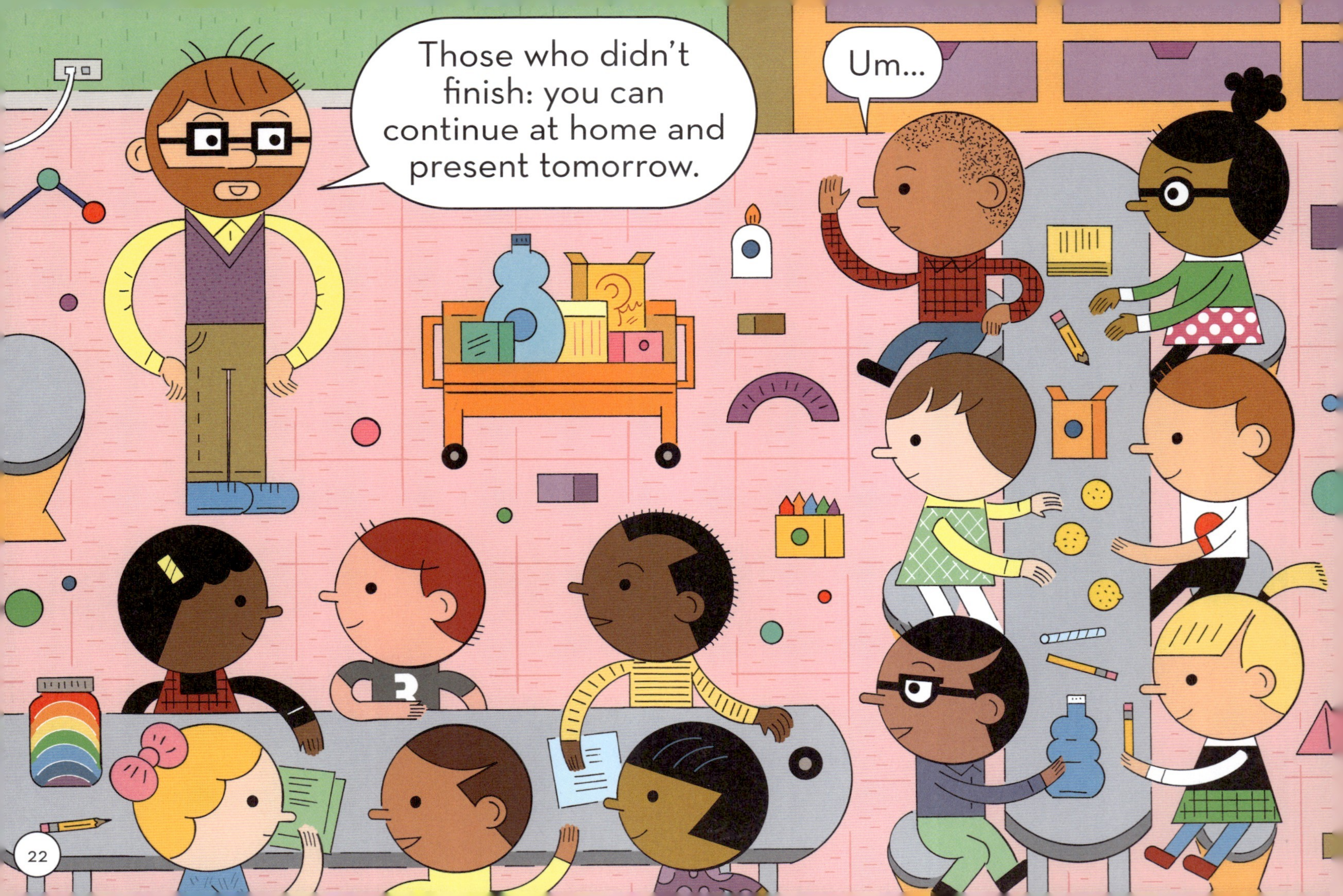
Those who didn't finish: you can continue at home and present tomorrow.
Um...

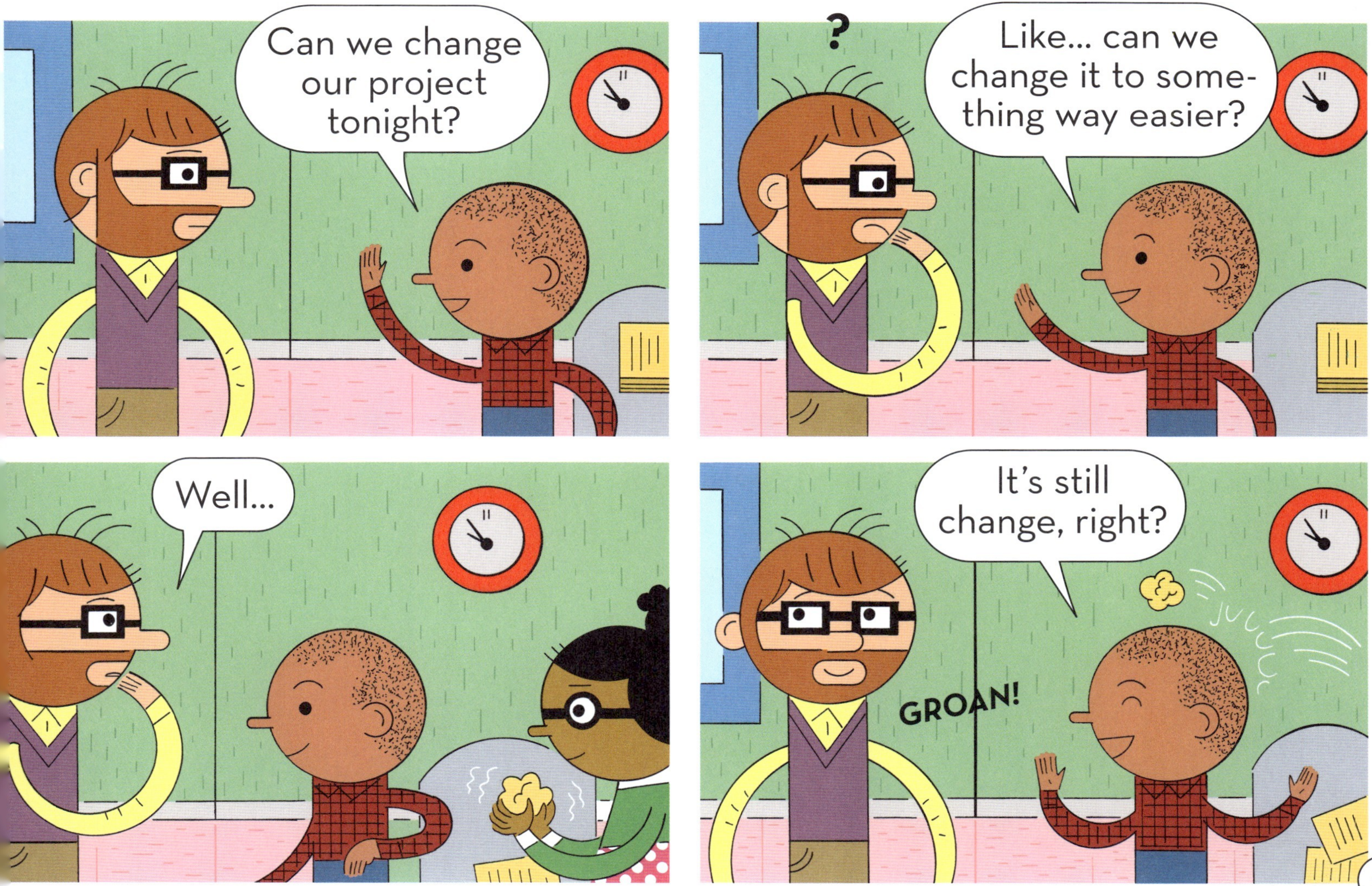
Can we change our project tonight?
?
Like... can we change it to some-thing way easier?
Well...
It's still change, right?
GROAN!

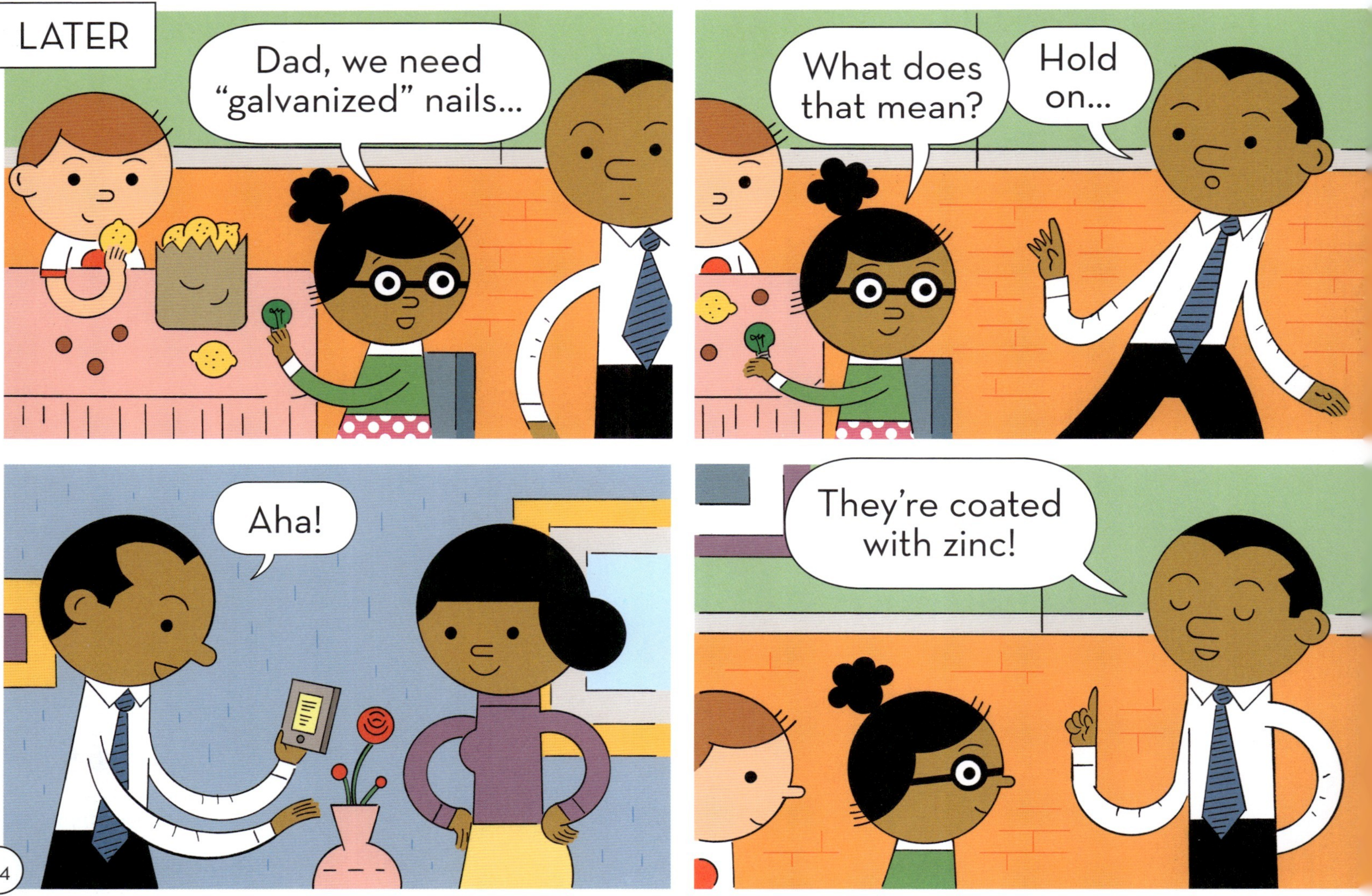
LATER
Dad, we need "galvanized" nails...
What does that mean?
Hold on...
Aha!
They're coated with zinc!

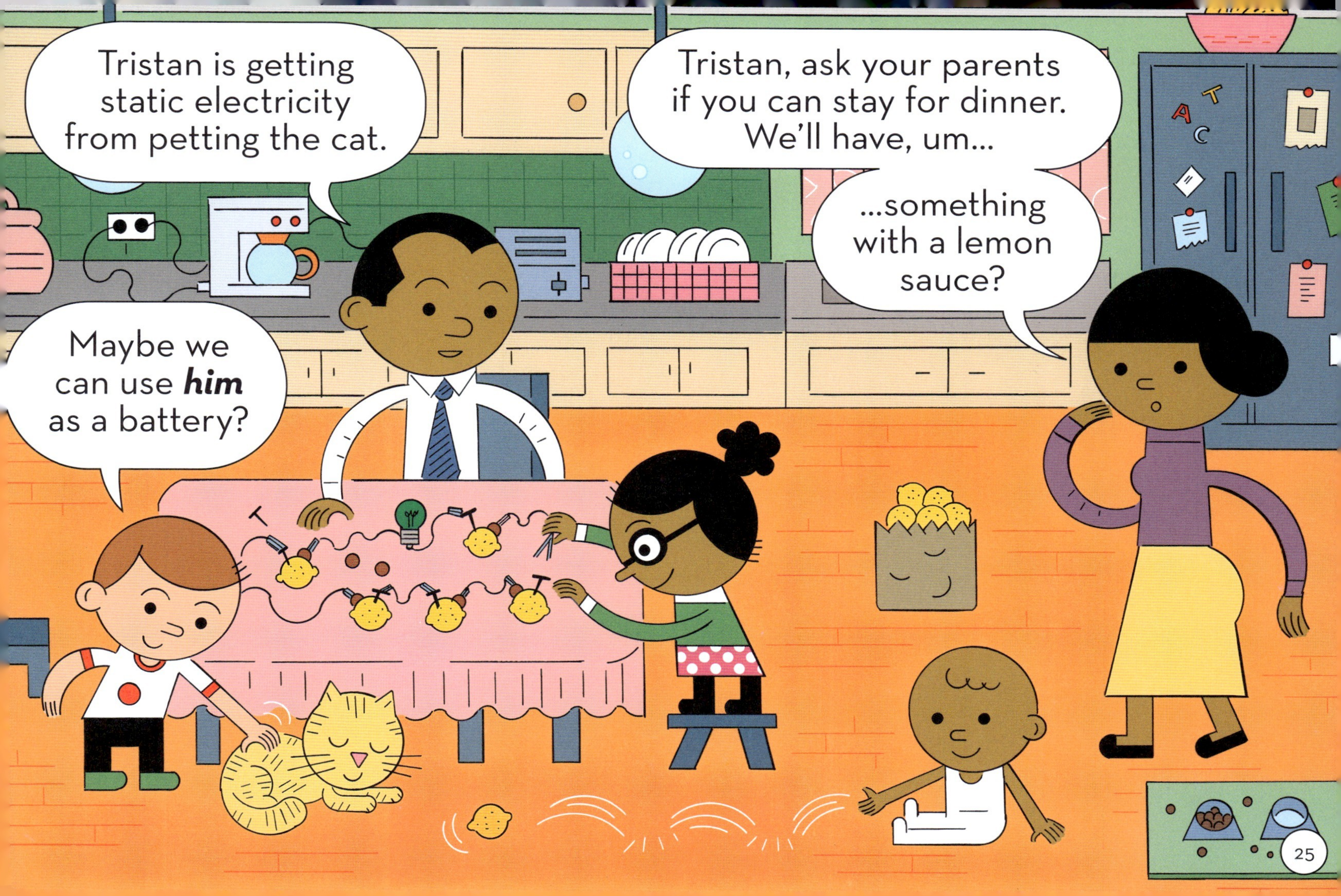
Tristan is getting static electricity from petting the cat.
Tristan, ask your parents if you can stay for dinner. We'll have, um...
...something with a lemon sauce?
Maybe we can use ***him*** as a battery?

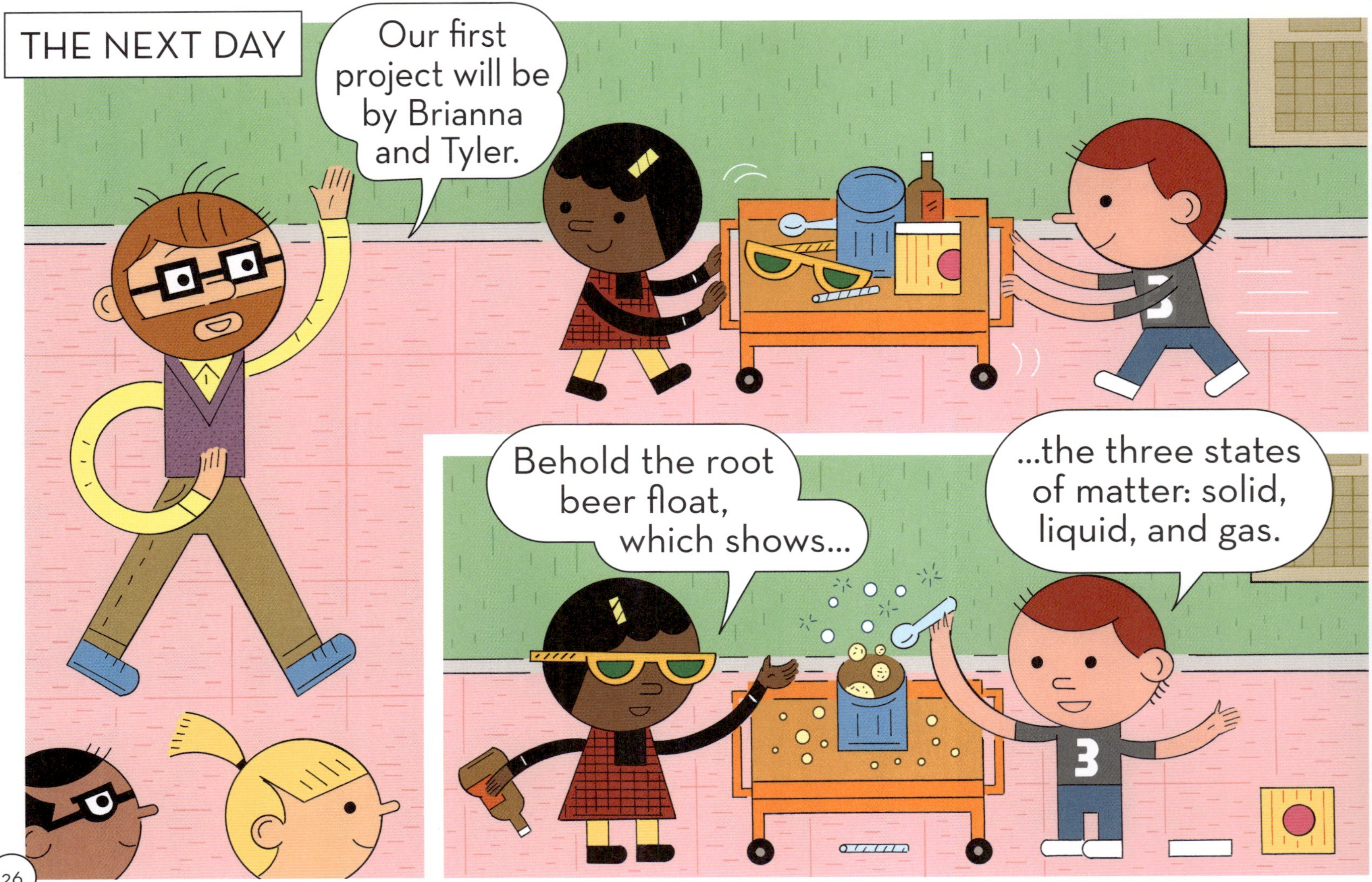
THE NEXT DAY
Our first project will be by Brianna and Tyler.
Behold the root beer float, which shows...
...the three states of matter: solid, liquid, and gas.
3
3

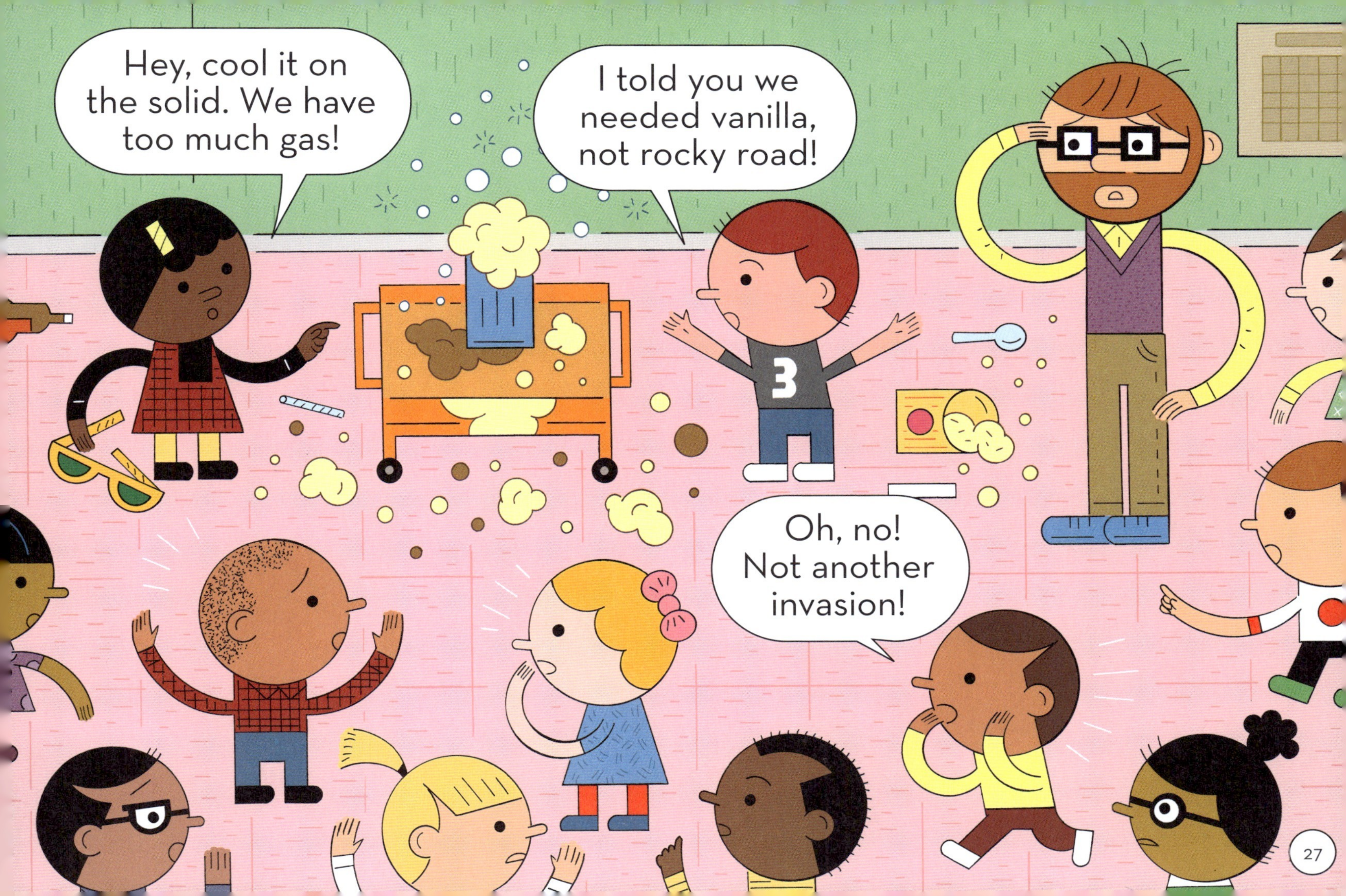
Hey, cool it on the solid. We have too much gas!
I told you we needed vanilla, not rocky road!
Oh, no! Not another invasion!

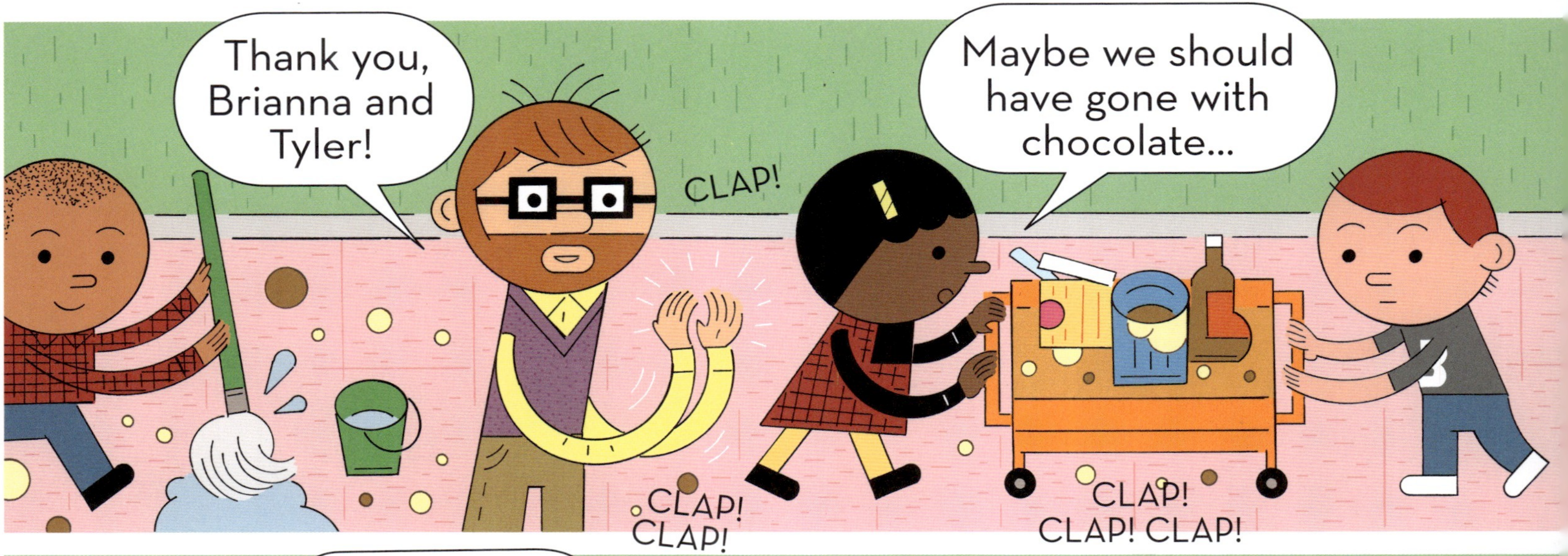
Thank you, Brianna and Tyler!
CLAP!
CLAP! CLAP!
Maybe we should have gone with chocolate...
CLAP! CLAP! CLAP!

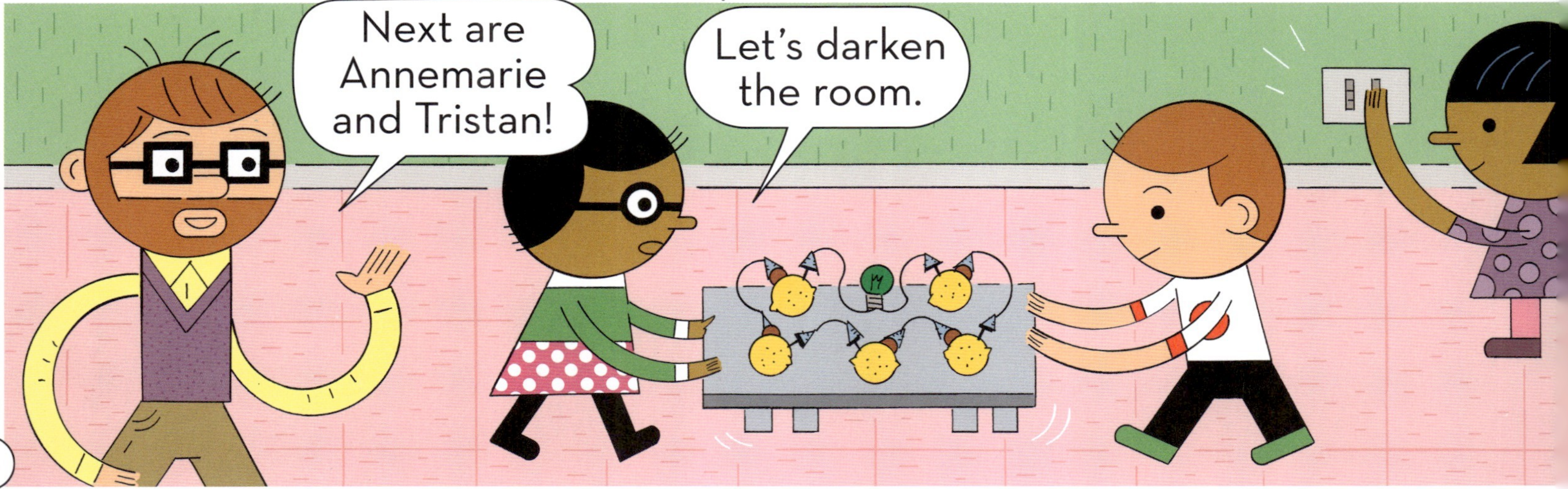
Next are Annemarie and Tristan!
Let's darken the room.

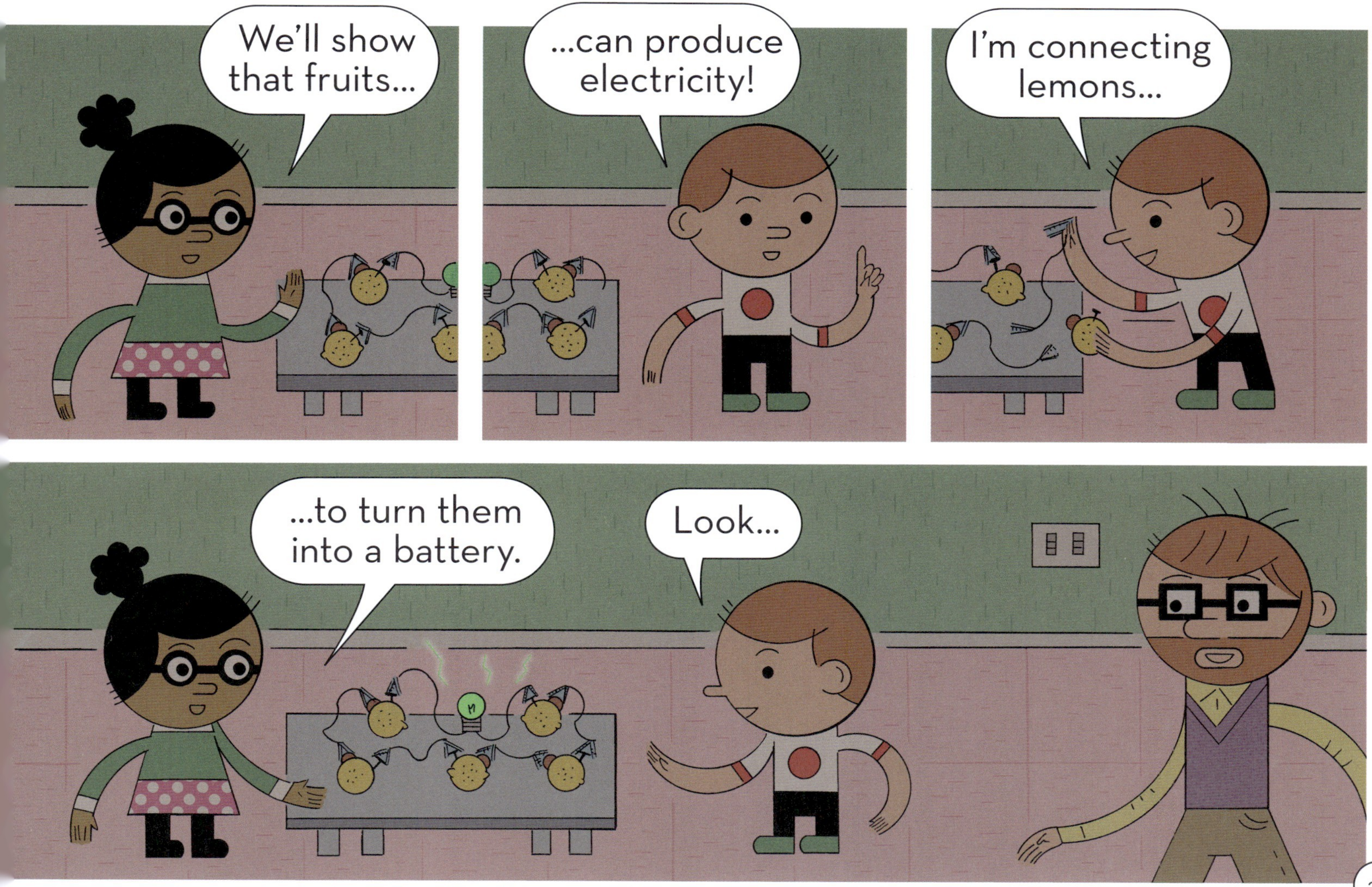
We'll show that fruits...
...can produce electricity!
I'm connecting lemons...
...to turn them into a battery.
Look...

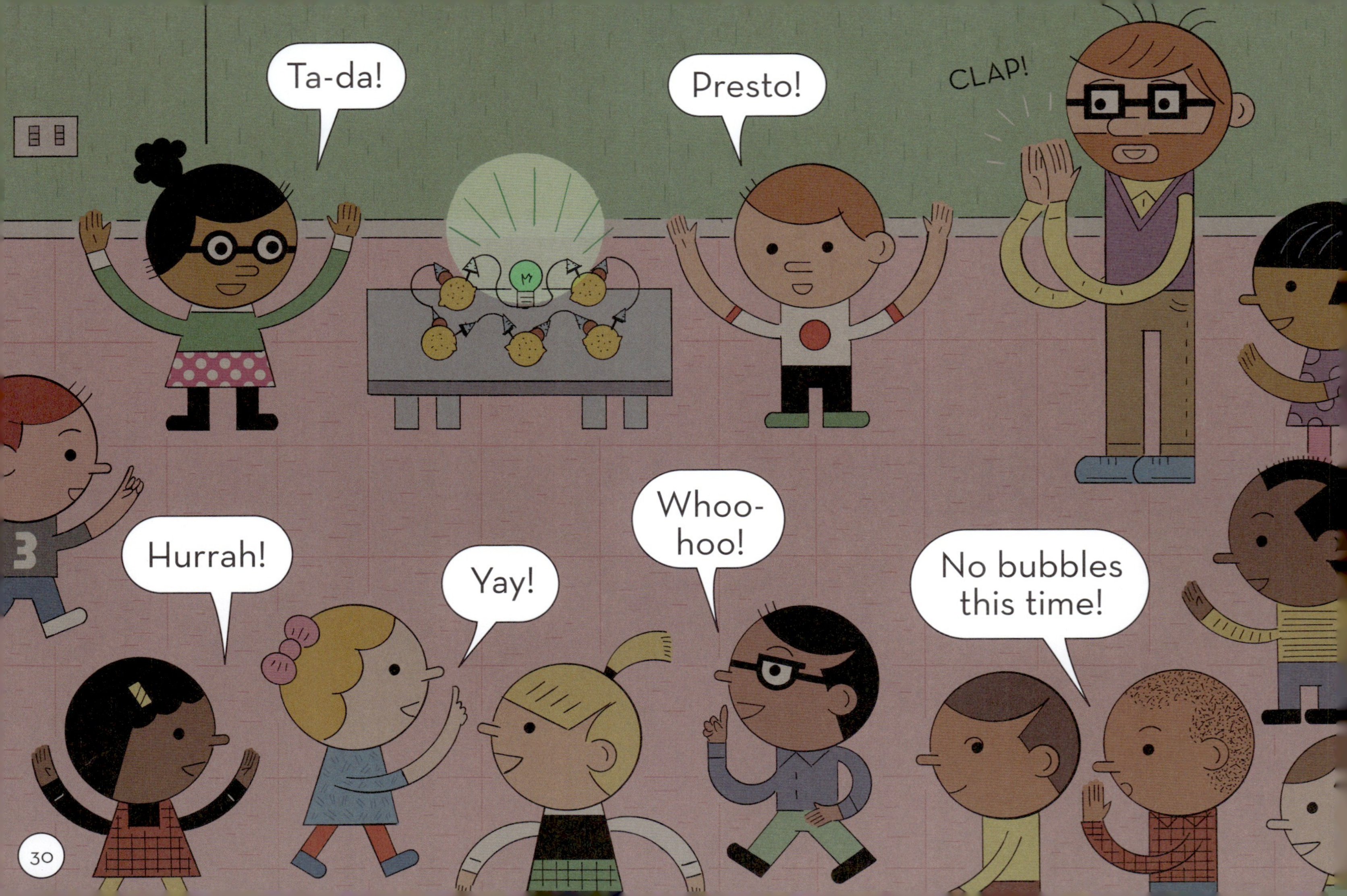
Ta-da!
Presto!
CLAP!
Hurrah!
Yay!
Whoo-hoo!
No bubbles this time!

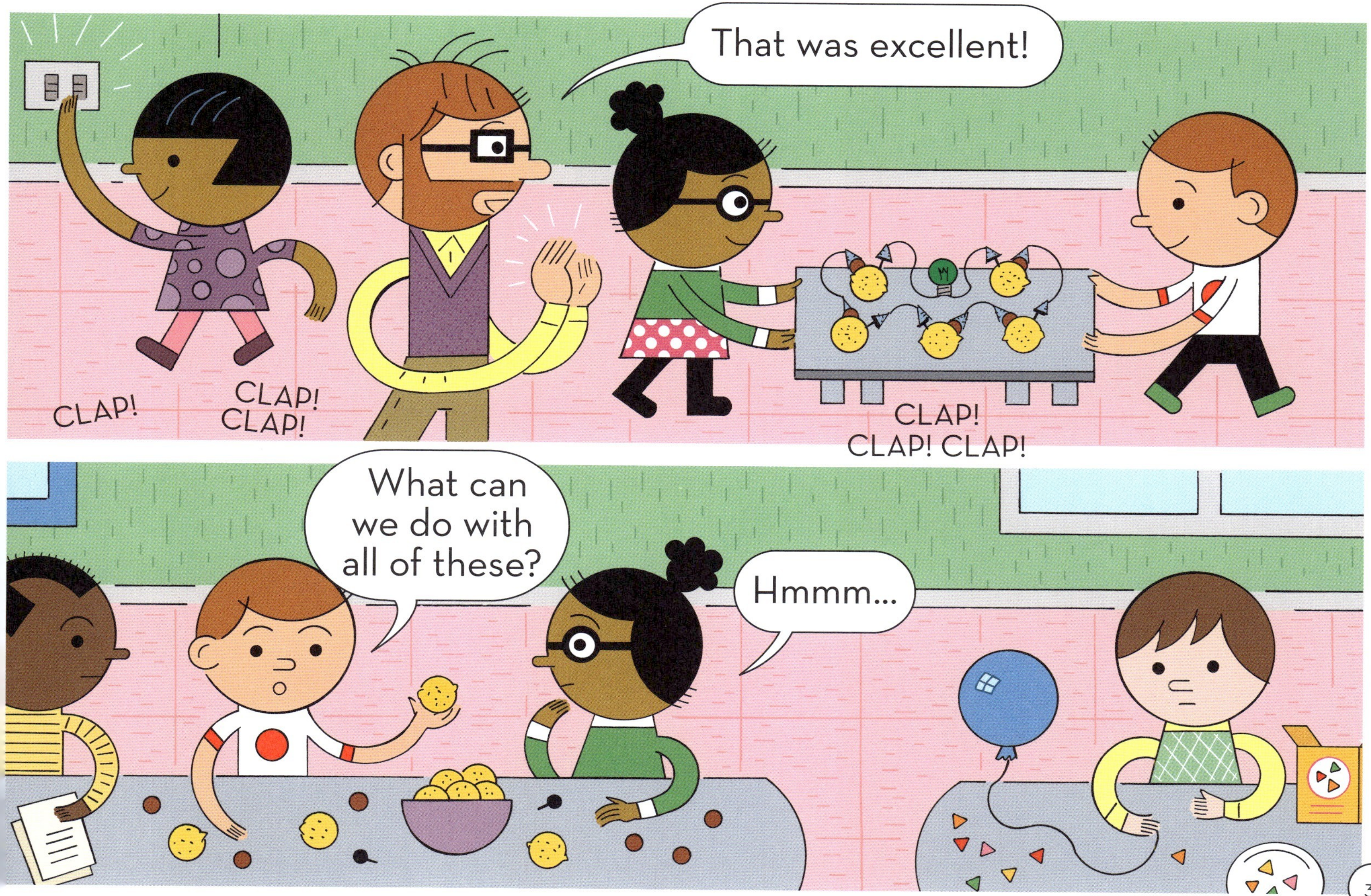
CLAP!
CLAP! CLAP!
That was excellent!
CLAP! CLAP! CLAP!
What can we do with all of these?
Hmmm...

ABOUT THE AUTHOR

IVAN BRUNETTI lives in Chicago and works as a teacher, an illustrator, and a cartoonist, usually in that order. He says: "As a kid, I would go to the library almost every day. I wanted to know how the world worked. Everything seemed so big, mysterious, and strange. It still does! I hope I never lose my sense of curiosity, because there is always more to discover. I may not be able to fix a toaster, but at least I can learn how people bake bread." He is the author of the highly praised TOON Books: **Wordplay**, **3x4**, **Shapes and Shapes**, and **Comics: Easy as ABC!** His work has appeared in the *New Yorker* and *New York Times*, among other publications.

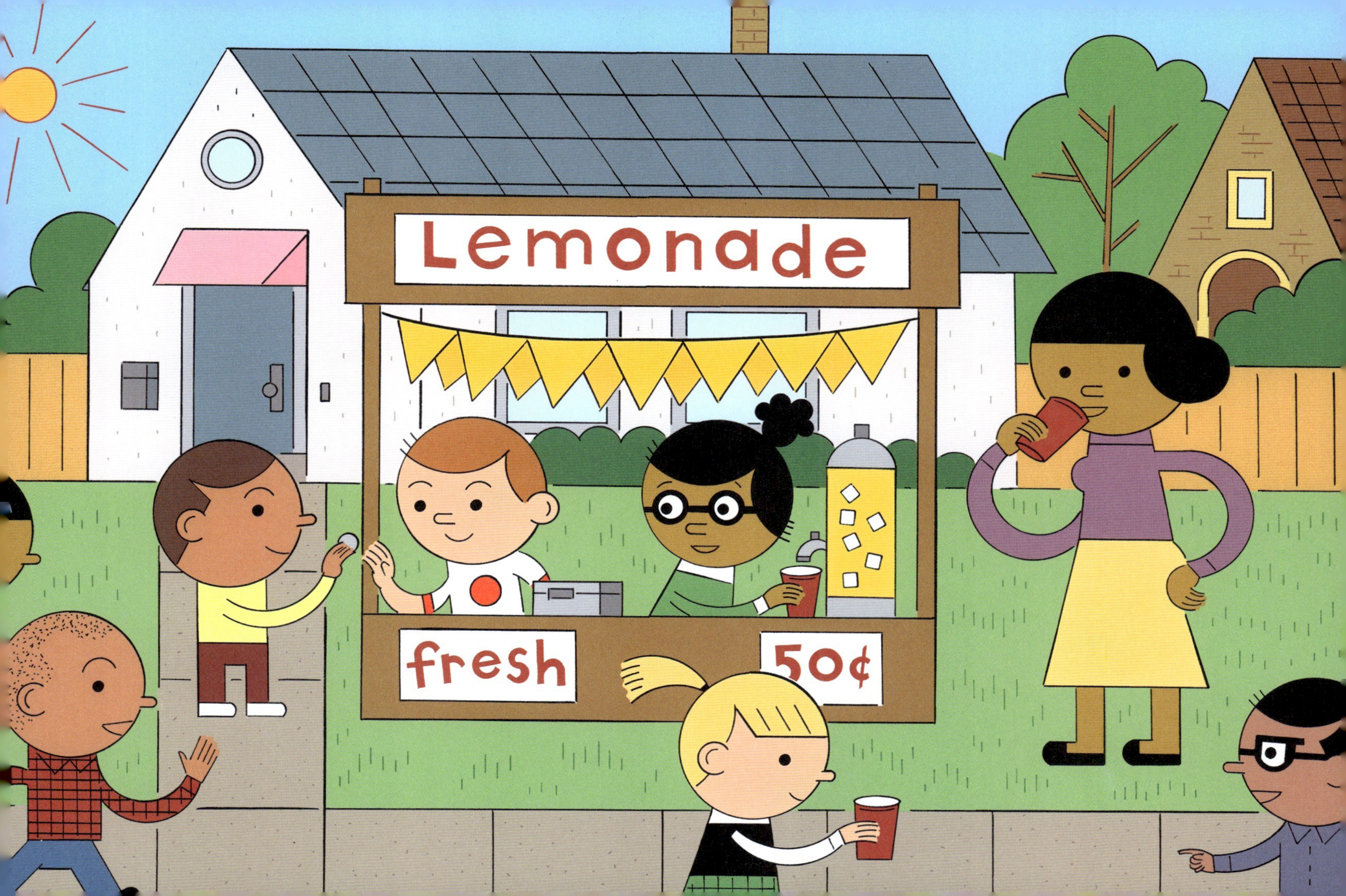
Lemonade
fresh
50¢

TIPS FOR PARENTS AND TEACHERS:
HOW TO READ COMICS WITH KIDS

Kids love comics! They are naturally drawn to the details in the pictures, which make them want to read the words. Comics beg for repeated readings and let both emerging and reluctant readers enjoy complex stories with a rich vocabulary. But since comics have their own grammar, here are a few tips for reading them with kids:

GUIDE YOUNG READERS: Use your finger to show your place in the text, but keep it at the bottom of the character speaking so it doesn't hide the very important facial expressions.

HAM IT UP! Think of the comic book story as a play, and don't hesitate to read with expression and intonation. Assign parts or get kids to supply the sound effects, a great way to reinforce phonics skills.

LET THEM GUESS: Comics provide lots of context for the words, so emerging readers can make informed guesses. Like jigsaw puzzles, comics ask readers to make connections, so check children's understanding by asking, "What's this character thinking?" (But don't be surprised if a kid finds some of the comics' subtle details faster than you.)

TALK ABOUT THE PICTURES: Point out how the artist paces the story with pauses (silent panels) or speeded-up action (a burst of short panels). Discuss how the size and shape of the panels convey meaning.

ABOVE ALL, ENJOY! There is of course never one right way to read, so go for the shared pleasure. Once children make the story happen in their imagination, they have discovered the thrill of reading, and you won't be able to stop them. At that point, just go get them more books—and more comics!

www.TOON-BOOKS.com
SEE OUR FREE ONLINE CARTOON MAKERS, LESSON PLANS, AND MUCH MORE